Day out of Days

STORIES

SAM SHEPARD

VINTAGE BOOKS

A DIVISION OF RANDOM HOUSE, INC.

NEW YORK

FIRST VINTAGE BOOKS EDITION, FEBRUARY 2011

Some of the stories in this work originally appeared in the following:
"Indianapolis" and "Land of the Living" in *The New Yorker*;
"Costello," "Cracker Barrel Men's Room," "Majesty," and "Van Horn, Texas"
in *The Paris Review*; and "Thor's Day" in *Zoetrope: All-Story*.

Grateful acknowledgment is made to W.W. Norton & Company, Inc. for
permission to reprint an excerpt from "Degrees of Gray in Philipsburg" from
Making Certain It Goes On: The Collected Poems of Richard Hugo.
Reprinted by permission of W.W. Norton & Company, Inc.

The Library of Congress has cataloged the Knopf edition as follows:
Shepard, Sam.
Day out of days: stories / Sam Shepard.—1st ed.
p. cm.
I. Title.
PS3569.H394D39 2010
813'.54—dc22   2009019578

Vintage ISBN: 978-0-307-27782-4

Book design by Virginia Tan

www.vintagebooks.com

Printed in the United States of America
10 9 8 7 6 5 4 3 2 1

"His literary voice . . . [is] strong, unpretentious, and singular. . . . He writes with the kind of authority that makes you believe— and with the kind of depth that makes you think." —Elle.com

"Mournfully funny. . . . Well-observed. . . . As a collection of tiny jewels of language unearthed with great care by a man with a uniquely American voice, it's unlike anything else."
—*The Onion*

"Read [it] the way the faithful may read their Bibles: a few verses nightly to serve as inspiration, and a shield from despair."
—*The L Magazine*

"No one writes like Shepard or better captures the fallout from American myths: of freedom, entitlement and masculinity."
—*The Post and Courier*

"Powerfully entertaining." —*Richmond Times-Dispatch*

"Gripping and elusive at the same time. . . . Dark and weirdly funny. . . . There's something about Shepard that invites awe. Sam Shepard is Samuel Beckett as Marlboro Man. . . . Readers of Hemingway, Cormac McCarthy, Jim Harrison and Thomas McGuane will recognize the type." —*The Hartford Advocate*

"Always there's the tremendous poetry of Shepard's language."
—*The Oregonian*

"Moving. . . . Again and again, we find in *Day out of Days*, everything in life is a mystery; the road to answers, or even a satisfying sense of place, never ends." —*Chicago Sun-Times*

SAM SHEPARD

Day out of Days

Sam Shepard is the Pulitzer Prize–winning author of more than forty-five plays. As an actor, he has appeared in more than thirty films, and he received an Oscar nomination in 1984 for *The Right Stuff*. He was a finalist for the W. H. Smith Literary Award for his story collection *Great Dream of Heaven*. He lives in New York and Kentucky.

Day out of Days

To all my family
and those long gone

That's the mistake I made . . . to have wanted a
story for myself, whereas life alone is enough.

—BECKETT

Contents

Contents

Contents

Contents

Contents

Contents

Deepest thanks to the following:

Rudy Wurlitzer

Michael Almereyda

Judy Boals

LuAnn Walther

Phil Gerow

Hal Jennings

Val Kilmer

Larry Shainberg

Rosemary Quinn

Patti

and Jessica

Day out of Days

Kitchen

I've always done my best work in the kitchen. I don't know why. Cooking stuff up. Maybe that's it. Now I've got my own kitchen deep in the country with a big round table smack in the middle. But I am surrounded. I'm not sure who put all this stuff in here. Who jumbled all this up on my white brick walls as though it told some story, made some sense; some whole world out of floating fractured bits and pieces. Pencil drawing of Seattle Slew, long after retirement—bloated pasture-belly, glazed far-off stare in his eye as though looking back to the glory days of the Triple Crown. And, wedged between the glass and flat black frame, snapshots of different sons in different shirts doing different things like fishing, riding mules and tractors; leaning up against their different mothers at radical angles. Postcards of nineteenth-century Lakota warriors like Gaul, adopted son of Sitting Bull, price on his head; left for dead only to come back and seek his perfect vengeance at the Battle of the Little Bighorn. Henry Miller with a walking stick, black beret, sitting on a rock wall gesticulating to the camera, some quote about morality and why don't we just give ourselves over completely and unabashedly to the present, since we're all up against the same grim prospect anyway; same sinking ship. Slaves in sepia tone, harvesting bluegrass seed and whistling "Dixie." Wedged between the tile and brick, more pix of hawks and galloping horses out near where we used to chase skinny coyotes back into the tangled mesquite and ocotillo. Then Beckett's sorrowful bespectacled hawk-face, gazing into oblivion with no trace of self-pity, resigned, hands clasped between his knees. Underneath in

3

neat black scrawl: "There is no return game between a man and his stars."

Who scrambled all this stuff in here with no seeming regard for associative order, shape, or color? Without the slightest care for where it might all wind up. Just randomly pinned to cupboards and door frames, slipping sideways; gathering spotted stove grease and fly shit. El Santuario de Chimayó, for instance, caked in Christmas snow, but what's it doing right next door to a business card for my horseshoer with an anvil and hammer logo? Then, working up the wall, there's the little bay in Lubec, Maine, where another set of rum-running ancestors lay long buried, then magic stones from Bernalillo, Wounded Knee, the painted stick, guts of the dream catcher, antelope, prairie dog, old speckled racing grey-hounds flying off the tailgates; rusted spurs on the back of the black walnut door. What's all this shit for? Some display for who? For me? What for? Some guest or other? I have no guests. You know that. I'm no host. Never have been. Maybe the old Sonoran man who drops off split oak but no real visitors, that's for sure. Everyone knows to stay far away. Especially now with the tiger-brindled pit bull out front. The screaming burro kicking buckets down the hill. The fighting gallo in attack mode. I'm in this bunker all my own, surrounded by mysterious stuff. It may be time to take a break and walk back out into the dripping black woods where I know the hollowed-out Grandaddy Sycamore sits and waits for you to climb inside and breathe up into its bone-white aching arms.

Haskell, Arkansas

(Highway 70)

Sunday, midday. Not many cars. Man's out for a stroll. He comes across a head in a ditch by the side of the road; walks right past it, thinking he hasn't seen what he's just seen; thinking it's not possible. He stops. His heart starts picking up a little. His breath gets choppy. He's shaking now and he's never understood why his body always takes over in moments of panic like this; why his body refuses to listen to his head. He turns and goes back. He stops again and stares down into the ditch. There it is. Big as life. He's staring straight at it. A severed head in a wicker basket. He picks up a stick and pokes it like he's done before with dead dogs or deer. The skin puffy and blue and the eyes shut tight, squinting as though frozen in the moment of amputation. The head sporting a Pancho Villa–style moustache; two buckteeth slightly visible; a single spot of blood on the lower lip. No other signs of gore. No dangling arteries or purple mess. It's a cleanly decapitated head resting flat in the bottom of a basket with what looks like burlap tucked neatly around the abbreviated neck. Black locks of matted hair dangle in snaky coils down both ears. The body is nowhere in sight. The man is relieved about that. In fact, he hopes he doesn't stumble across it in the same way he came across the head. That might be more than he could handle at this point.

Suddenly, the head starts to speak to the man in a soft, lilting voice. The eyes of the head don't open; the lips don't move. The voice just seems to be floating out the top of the skull. It's a humble, quiet kind of voice with no accent that the man can make out. Maybe the islands. The head asks the man if he'll kindly pick up the basket and carry it to a place it would prefer to be. A tranquil place not too far from here, away from the pounding sun and the roar of traffic. The head tells the man it's been hard for him to think straight in this miserable ditch. Panic takes hold of the man and he runs. He runs so fast and desperately that he quickly exhausts himself and falls down flat on his face. He hasn't fallen so completely flat as this since he was a little kid running away from his father; running for his life. With his teeth in the dirt the man hears the head calling out to him in the most forlorn and melancholy voice the man has ever heard. It makes his whole heart ache. The man pulls himself up off the ground, spitting little grains of sand. He turns and returns to the head. He can't help himself. His heart is pounding wildly. He tells the head he doesn't want to be involved; this was purely accidental, this meeting between the two of them, and he wants to just continue on his way as though the whole thing never happened. The head pleads with the man and the voice of the head is so full of yearning that the man remains rooted to the ground. The head tells him he's been calling out for days to the passing cars but no one hears him, no one stops. The man is the first one to stop. This makes the man feel important somehow; the idea that he might be some kind of hero. He likes that idea and his heart begins to relax and return to normal. The man asks the head, very tentatively, where it is he might want to be taken and the head answers, "A lake, not too far from here. It won't take very long. You can just throw me into the flat water and then be on your way." The man considers for a moment then agrees to carry the head on one condition and that is that the head will please not speak to him anymore other than to give him simple clear directions on how to get to the lake and, above all, he should never again make that mournful, melancholy sound. The head agrees eagerly to all this and immediately goes silent.

When the man bends over to pick up the head in the basket he discovers it's much heavier than he would have imagined. It must weigh fifty pounds or more. Dead weight. The head laughs then quickly stops itself, not wanting to anger the man; not wanting the man to think he's being made fun of. The man hoists the basket up to his waist and carries the head a few yards on his hip, like a mother would carry an infant, then sets it down, panting and gasping. The head laughs in spite of itself and the man becomes angry, just as the head had anticipated. "What's so funny?" demands the man but the head won't answer. The man immediately storms off feeling that he's been the brunt of some joke. The head calls out again in the most heartbreaking, plangent voice the man has ever heard. It stops him cold in his tracks. "You promised me you wouldn't make that awful sound again!" the man screams.

"I'm sorry," says the head, "but it's the only way to get your attention." The man walks reluctantly back to the head and stops in front of it. He feels now that he's hooked on this head. He stares down at it. The head is silent again. The eyes remain closed and squinting tight. There seems to be no life in the head at all. The man knows different. "How did you get separated from your body?" asks the man point-blank. This is the question that's been haunting him.

"I was beheaded," says the head.

"How?" asks the man.

"By a gleaming silver saber," says the head.

"But who held the saber? Who brought it down on your neck?"

"I never saw it coming," says the head.

"But you must have known it was coming," says the man.

"Yes, but it didn't help."

"What?" says the man.

"Knowing. Knowing didn't help."

"So, you have no idea who it might have been?" asks the man.

"I have many ideas but it doesn't matter now."

"Don't you want to seek your vengeance?" asks the man. The head starts laughing and can't stop. "Don't laugh at me!" screams the man. The head stops. "I can't stand that," says the man. "All my life I've been laughed at."

"I'm sorry," says the head.

"I can't carry you, that's for sure. You're way too heavy," says the man and the head begins to weep. Tears roll out of the squinting eyes.

"Don't do that," says the man. "I can't stand it if you do that."

"You're my only chance," says the head, trying to control itself.

"You're way heavier than I expected," insists the man.

"Just try lifting the basket up to your shoulder. It's much easier that way."

"I can't," says the man.

"You can't or you won't?" asks the head.

"I can't."

"You must," says the head.

"Why must I? I don't even know you! You can't just start ordering me around. I'm doing you a favor!"

"You owe it to yourself," says the head.

"What!" exclaims the man, turning his back on the head altogether. "I'm just walking along here on Highway 70, minding my own business, like I do every Sunday afternoon about this time, and I happen to stumble across a head in a basket and now you're telling me what I owe myself! You don't even know me!"

"All the more reason," says the head.

"All the more reason, what!" shouts the man.

"All the more reason you should take it upon yourself."

"I'm not following you," says the man.

"You owe me your life," says the head and the man freezes.

"What?" says the man.

"You heard me," says the head. "If you walk away and abandon me, you will pay the price," and now the voice of the head has dropped several octaves and taken on a gravity that is truly shocking to the man's central nervous system. He can feel the highway tremble beneath him. His breath quickens and his mouth goes dry.

"What's that supposed to mean?" asks the man, his voice quavering like grass in the wind.

"Turn your back on me and you will find out," says the head. The man stands there staring up and down the nearly empty highway. He feels as though his knees are about to buckle. Far off, in the village he can hear the chimes of the Episcopal church playing "Onward, Christian Soldiers." He knows the tune well. He remembers being a choirboy in that same church. A lime-green Camaro goes flashing by. Bald teenagers with snakes tattooed around their mouths are yelling insults at him out the windows. A bottle of Coors Light goes whizzing past his cheekbone. The man now begins to feel as though *he* is the abandoned one and not the head. He feels as though he could make the same terrible mournful moan that the head was making but nothing comes out. No sound at all, just a terrified rasping like a lost animal. The man wonders how he could be so suddenly separated from his former life, his former self. And then an even deeper terror wells up that he can't remember ever having a former life. Who was he, first thing this morning after coffee, stepping out the door on the way toward this Sunday stroll?

"All right!" says the man abruptly, as though to shake himself out of this terrible doubt. "I'll try it, I'll try carrying you, just for a while," and he hoists the head in the basket up to his hip again and then with a tremendous grunt heaves the basket up to his shoulder where he teeters precariously like an Olympic weight lifter. The head mimics the sound of a gigantic crowd roaring approval. It sounds absolutely realistic. The man has the impression again that the head is making fun of him but proceeds nevertheless, weaving with the weight of it; basket on his shoulder going in the direction the head has proclaimed.

"You're doing very well," the head says sincerely. "I'm proud of you."

"Don't try to butter me up," says the man. "You don't even know me."

"I know you better than you know yourself," says the head.

"Who are you!" demands the man.

"Never mind about that. Just keep following the road." The man is wobbling badly. The cords in his neck are burning from the weight. His sides are heaving. He's not used to this kind of labor. He's grown accustomed to a soft, passive existence where nothing happens, nothing counts; where no single day ever stands out more than any other single day; where dreaming and waking all run together; where all the people in his life have disappeared and his main pursuits are napping and watching Mexican soap operas cast with dark-haired weeping beauties and the fantasies they evoke. He suddenly collapses under a concrete viaduct and drops the basket beside him. The head rolls out and comes to rest with the black gaping hole of the severed neck sticking straight up. The man stares into the hole, gasping for air, and listens to the voice of the head speaking very calmly: "We just need to make a right turn here, after the bridge, and then follow the irrigation ditch. It's not very far."

"I can't," protests the man. "I've had enough now! I'm going to leave you here." The head screams and begins to weep again and the sound of it makes the man's whole body quake. He feels as though he's been struck by lightning.

"Don't do that, please," says the man. "I'm begging you. I can't take it. I've told you that. The sound of your weeping and moaning reminds me of everything I want to forget. Everything I've put to death in order to go on."

"Then, finish carrying me to the lake," says the head.

"I don't think I'm physically capable," says the man. "It's not that I don't want to, it's just that— I can't."

"Then, turn me over at least," says the head.

"What?"

"Turn me right side up."

"I'm not going to touch you," says the man.

"Just nudge me with your knee."

"What?"

"Nudge me with your knee. I'll roll right over." The man musters his courage and nudges the black neck of the head with his knee and the head rolls over, right side up, just as the head implied. "Now put me back in the basket, please."

"I'm not going to touch you!" repeats the man. "You keep talking me into these things against my will."

"Are you afraid that if you touch me you might disappear?"

"What's that supposed to mean?" asks the man.

"You might cross the line? Pass out and never return to your body?"

"You're the one with no body," says the man.

"Exactly," says the head. "Now, just grab me by the hair and drop me back in the basket, please."

"No!" shouts the man. "I'm not grabbing you by the hair! It would be like taking hold of a handful of snakes." Again, the head releases his doleful wail and, before the man even realizes what he's doing, he's snatched the head up by the hair and plopped it back in the basket.

"That wasn't so bad, was it?" says the head. "I'm deeply grateful."

"You're like a spoiled child," says the man indignantly.

"I'm like nothing you've ever come across," says the head.

"Well, it's nothing to be proud of," says the man.

"Pick me up once more," says the head. "And this time lift me all the way up to the top of your head and carry me up there."

"Are you crazy?" says the man. "I can't possibly lift you all the way up to the top of my head. I could barely carry you on my hip."

"Yes, you can," says the head. "Just make one tremendous effort. Make an effort like you've never made before in your entire life. As though it were a matter of life and death."

"I don't have it in me," says the man. "Those days are long gone."

"Stand up and give it a whirl," says the head. "Be a man."

"Are you intentionally insulting me?" asks the man.

"I'm offering you a chance to be."

"I've got nothing to prove," says the man.

"Then go away and leave me alone," says the head abruptly.

"That's what I've been trying to do all along," says the man. "Since the moment I met you."

"Do it," says the head. "See if you can. Just walk away."

"You threatened me before. You said I would pay the price if I turned my back on you."

"There'll be no repercussions," says the head. "Believe me. Just walk away."

And now the man feels more alone than he's ever felt in his life. A deep, crushing aloneness that presses down through his chest. It's the very same feeling he's been trying to avoid since he was a little boy. The feeling he shakes off every morning when he stumbles toward his toothbrush and every night when he clicks off the light. Without thinking, he reaches down and grabs the handles of the wicker basket and with a mighty heave swings the head up to his shoulder and then, with a final grunt, manages to place the basket on top of his head. He has no idea how he's accomplished this all at once but feels suddenly all right about himself; as though the sun has just popped out from behind the clouds.

"Now we're going to look like a man with two heads staggering down the highway," says the man to the head. "One on top of the other."

"We *are* a man with two heads," says the head brightly from his lofty perch.

"No," says the man. "We're two separate things. You don't belong to me. I just found you by the side of the road. Don't forget that."

"Whatever you like," says the head. "Keep straight ahead. I can see the lake from here."

"What's it look like?" asks the man.

"Flat. Green. Absolutely peaceful."

"Is it what you were hoping for?" says the man.

"We'll see when we get there," answers the head.

Chatter

I now have an almost constant swirling chatter going on inside my head from dawn to dusk. I never could have foreseen this when I was five, playing with sticks in the dirt, but I guess it's been slowly accumulating over all these sixty-some years; growing more intense, less easy to ignore. I wake up with it. I feed chickens with it. I drive tractors with it. I make coffee with it. I fry eggs with it. I ride horses with it. I go to bed with it. I sleep with it. It is my constant companion.

Sometimes I'm casually talking to people; looking them earnestly in the eye; just people in town, down at the Jot 'Em Down grocery store buying the *Racing Form,* dog food, half-and-half; wondering if they too might have a constant chattering going on inside *their* heads. We could be talking about anything; the breakdown of the gray filly in the Kentucky Derby, the rising price of corn; it doesn't matter, I continue to wonder the whole time. I have no idea what it's really like with other people. Actually, I have no idea what it's really like with me, when you get right down to it. I'm fishing in the dark.

Sometimes, though, I can clearly hear voices I don't recognize at all. Strangers. I've never heard them before. Voices conjured from water running in the sink, gurgling coffee, pissing in the creek, bacon frying, distant moaning highway trucks. They just appear; volunteer themselves, uninvited. I'm eavesdropping like— listening at the door to another room. Sometimes, they drop way off into the background and vanish. Something else takes their place. Some tone comes up. Some rhythm or other. Some tune. Sometimes, pure silence and my heart sings. Just like that it can happen. You're standing there in a blue field and everything suddenly stops. Miraculous. Then it all starts up again. Churning away.

Williams, Arizona

(Highway 40 West)

The actor wakes up. It's 6:45 a.m. Mountain Time according to his Indiglo Timex. He's staring at the sun-faded color blowup of the Grand Canyon mounted above the TV in a cheap frame. The picture's warped. The wall it hangs on is phony pink adobe. Actually, it's sheetrock with pink crud smeared on it like curdled Pepto-Bismol. The "Fun Things to Do in Williams" brochure propped up by the lamp on the bedside table, accompanied by yet another dizzying helicopter view of the deep gorge, reminds him that he has spent the night at the "Gateway to the Grand Canyon." The giant sun is just beginning to burn through the one window. The High Desert peeks in; yucca and candelaria. Now he remembers. He's on his way to L.A. to finish up some looping on a film he shot last summer. A film he cares nothing about anymore and can't remember why he wanted to do in the first place. A film he can't even remember the title of. Is that true? It must be, he says to himself. Yes, it's true. I can't remember the title. I have no idea. No inclination. He swings his very white legs out from under the Navajo print blanket and just sits on the edge of the mattress staring out the window for a while. He's trying to adjust. His eyes. His breath. He sees a low red bluff in the distance turning slowly to blaze orange. A crow flies languidly past. He pictures the same old route he's always taken east to west; down through Kansas City on 35, cutting across to Wichita, down to Tucumcari, picking up

40 West, paralleling the fabled and long-abandoned Route 66—the highway he grew up on. The highway that shaped his youth. He stands slowly, hoping his trick knee doesn't suddenly give out on him. He remembers the last news item on TV before he fell asleep. It just pops into his head. A very attractive blonde reporter with flashing teeth all excited about Special Forces closing in on Osama bin Laden somewhere near the Hindu Kush. Supposed sightings of an extremely tall figure dressed as a woman, riding a donkey over the mountain pass. Very biblical. Suspiciously vivid. They were sure they had him cornered. The CIA had reliable contacts, they said. They'd infiltrated the villages. He walks to the TV and flicks it on then heads to the narrow bathroom and throws water on his face. His face— He can't stand his face anymore. Pathetic—no longer young. A self-pitying shroud around the eyes and forehead. Widow's peak receding dramatically. Teeth (which never were his best asset) have grown gray and his disappearing gum line gives them the aura of wax fangs or an Appalachian miner's mouth. There's a stale breath stench too, which is a bad sign, he thinks. (He's always looking for signs.) He wonders if maybe it's an indication of some deeper internal disorder; something to do with the liver or lower intestine or maybe worse. What could that be? He shudders to think. There's a sharp voice from behind him that makes him jump and turn around. A punctilious female voice. He turns off the water to listen then remembers he'd left the TV on. He listens while he brushes his teeth, bearing down on the plaque ferociously. A woman is being interviewed by Larry King. What is it about Larry King's voice, he asks himself, that's so irritating? Something nasal in the treble clef. King is asking some hotshot woman reporter if it's true that she got a face-lift because a rival news network had offered her a better position if she improved her looks. She confesses that she went along with this proposition and doesn't regret it one bit. She likes her new face, her new career. He turns the water back on. He spits in the sink, rinses, and turns the faucet off. A semi roars down Highway 40, right outside the win-

dow. He goes back to the TV; changes channels searching for the bin Laden story but finds nothing but daytime talk shows, soap operas, cooking shows, Christian gospel shows, shows featuring pathetic victims of their own bad judgment, weeping and shameful screaming shows, repentance shows, violent cartoon shows, NASCAR shows, pornography shows, Spanish-language melodramas with gorgeous Mexican women in catfights shedding real tears, gay wrestling shows, knife collectors' auction shows, cheap-jewelry shows, Bible history shows, fat-people shows, diet shows, dog grooming shows, big-game shows with Cape buffalo being blown away on Texas ranches and crashing into the Brazos, motocross shows with spectacular wipeouts, flying burning metal in slow motion, windsurfing wrecks, deliberate car crashes into buildings and brick walls, gas fires blazing but nothing at all about a mysterious tall figure dressed as a woman riding a donkey across the Hindu Kush—the most wanted man on the face of the earth. It makes him want to quit show business altogether.

Duarte

Didn't we once have a freak show in Duarte? Wagons and rings. Right out on Highway 66 where the aqueduct begins. I remember the deep elephant smell. Peanuts in shells. The Petrified Man. Fat people poking him with pins. Only his eyes moved. The Two-Headed Calf. (Always a standby.) Bearded Lady Midget. Fetus in a Bottle. Human. Suspended. Drifting in strings of gooey yellow. Everything is coming back to me now. In Spanish.

Didn't we once have a Gypsy consultant in our linoleum kitchen? Is that what we called her? No. Couldn't have been. My dad believed in her, though. Before God. Before Mary. Poring through glossy High Desert brochures. Salton Sea. Preposterous mock-ups of golf courses seen through the irrigated mist of Rain Bird sprinklers. Jerry Lewis and Sinatra were supposed to appear. Him chain-smoking Old Golds. Shaking from whiskey. On the edge of which desert, he wanted to know. He got it confused with the Painted one. She couldn't say. Wouldn't. Why be so mysterious, I wondered. It's only land. Her pink bandana. Sulfur smell. Rubbing sage oil into her bony wrists and all the turquoise bracelets clacking like teeth. That was her, all right. Whatever we called her. Watching her through an open door collect her burro hobbled out in the orchard, chewing rotten avocados, pissing a hole in the dried-up leaves.

Wasn't there once a tall gray piano player too? Gentle. He came in a bright blue suit, haircut like a Fuller brush; played "Camptown Ladies" all through the night of Great-Aunt Gracie's death then later hanged himself in a Pasadena garage alongside his Chrysler sedan. I remember that now. Told stories of how Gracie was quite the Grande Dame; dated John Philip Sousa back in the day; seduced a Lumber Baron with her Blue Plate Special and captured hawks on weekends down in the Arroyo Seco. Everything's coming back to me now. In tiny pieces.

One Night in the Long-Ago

What happened, now? Are you telling me that this whole history of catastrophes is the result of one night in the long-ago?

That's what I understand.

The father came home late and smashed every window in the house with a claw hammer? Is that it?

That's what I heard.

Ripped the front door off its hinges and then set fire to the backyard?

So the story goes.

The son then snuck out one of the broken windows, under cover of dawn, with a few books in a paper sack?

So they say.

Day out of Days

Stepping over the unconscious, bleeding form of his father he then jumped into a Chevy and never stopped driving the rest his life?

That's it in a nutshell.

You'd think he'd be over it by, now, wouldn't you?

You'd think.

Indianapolis

(Highway 74)

I've been crisscrossing the country again, without much reason. Sometimes a place will just pop into my head and I'll take off. This time, down through Normal, Illinois, from high up in white Minnesota, dead of winter, icy roads, wind blowing sideways across the empty cornfields. Find myself stopping for the night outside Indianapolis, off 78, just before it makes its sweeping junction with 65 South to Louisville. I randomly pick a Holiday Inn, more for its familiar green logo and predictability than anything else. Plus, I'm wiped out. Evidently there's some kind of hot-rod convention going on in town, although I seem to remember those always taking place at the height of summer, when people can run around in convertible coupes with the tops down. Anyway, there are no rooms available except for possibly one and that one is "smoking," which I have nothing against. The desk clerk tells me she'd know in about ten minutes if there's going to be a cancellation. I'm welcome to wait, so I do, not wanting to face another ninety-some miles down to Kentucky through threatening weather.

I collapse into one of the overly stuffed sofas in the lobby, facing two plasma-screen TVs in opposing corners, both tuned to the same "reality" channel showing reruns of surveillance footage from convenience-store holdups: teenagers in hooded sweatshirts, one hand holding up their baggy jeans while the other pumps nine-millimeter slugs into screaming victims, who claim they have no access to the safe. I ask the desk clerk if she can please turn the

TVs off, or change the channel, but she says she has no control over any of it. The TVs are on some kind of preordained computer system, much like sprinklers in Los Angeles or security garage lights everywhere else. I ask her if she can at least mute the sound so I don't have to listen to the agonized groans of the victims or the raging insanity of the gunmen, but she says that she has no control over that either. I pick up a travel magazine off the glass table and leaf through it, pausing at every picture with a bikini-clad woman lounging beachside holding tall icy cocktails and staring smugly at the camera. The screams and groans and gunfire from the TVs keep repeating in looped cycles and soon lose all sense of being connected to murder. I find myself anticipating the next scream the way you would a familiar lyric in a pop song. (Here comes the high, shrieking temper-tantrum sequence just after he pops off a spray of four rapid shots.) I'm not sure how long I hang there in limbo in the lobby but it feels like way more than ten minutes.

A tall, skinny woman in a cloth Pat Nixon–type coat and a blue bandana comes through the revolving doors, pulling a small suitcase on wheels. She smiles at me as she passes and I feel immediately sad for no reason that I can put my finger on. She pauses at the desk to get her key, then continues on toward the elevators, giving me a quick glance over her shoulder as she disappears down the hallway. Again, I felt this little stab of melancholy, or maybe emptiness, maybe that's it. I stand and stretch, then walk over to the desk and ask the girl if she knows anything more about the cancellation. Not yet, she says, but reassures me that the possible guests will be calling any second now. They're coming in from Tupelo, Mississippi, everything depends on the weather, she says. I return to the squashy sofa and collapse again. (Isn't Tupelo where Elvis was born?) I notice the yellow spine of a *National Geographic* at the bottom of a stack and dig it out. The feature story is titled "The Black Pharaohs—Conquerors of Ancient Egypt." A man who looks very much like the young James Earl Jones is depicted on the cover; muscular arms crossed over his chest, with a leopard-skin cape, thick gold necklaces, and a gold-leaf skullcap with two shining falcons on the crown, staring stoically out. I am flipping through the glossy pages when I feel a tall presence beside me and a high-pitched female voice saying my name with a question mark behind it: "Stuart?" I turn to see the same skinny woman in her cloth coat but without the suitcase.

"You don't remember me, do you?" she asks. I stare into her green eyes searching for something to recognize, but the same tinge of melancholy is all I find. "Nineteen sixty-five," she says with a little sigh. "Tenth Street and Second Avenue? St. Mark's Church."

"I'm drawing a blank," I confess. "I've been driving for days. What seems like days, anyway."

She laughs nervously, half embarrassed, then stares at the carpet. "We lived together for a while. Don't you remember? We'd get up every morning and sit on the edge of my mattress eating bowls of wheat germ with brown honey all over it."

"Oh," I say, and keep staring into her with mounting desperation, wondering if maybe I've snapped some fragile synapse in my brain from too much driving. The final breakdown of road madness. Right here in Indianapolis. Then she does an amazing thing. She whips off the blue bandana and shakes out a mane of red hair that topples almost to her waist. Now it all comes back. "Oh—it's you," I say, still unable to attach a name.

"Who?" She giggles. "You don't remember me at all, do you?"

"Of course I do."

"You're just saying that."

"No—"

"Then what's my name? Come on, it wasn't that long ago."

"Nineteen sixty-five," I say.

"Or six—"

"No, it couldn't have been."

"Maybe sixty-eight. That was it."

"That's still forty years ago!"

"No!" She laughs.

"Add it up."

"Yeah, I guess it was, wasn't it?"

"Beth, right?" I blurt out.

"No, see? You don't remember."

"Betty?"

"Close."

"What then? This is wearing me out."

"Becky!" she announces with a beaming smile and her arms wide open as if I'm going to jump up and embrace her.

"Sure—Becky. That's right. Becky— Of course."

"What's my last name?"

"Oh, please— I can't keep up with this. I'm really wiped out—"

"Thane," she continues.

"Thane?"

"Thane. Becky Marie Thane."

"Right," I say.

"You really don't have any recollection at all, do you?" she says in almost a whisper, then stifles a little chuckle. She crosses her long arms and holds her shoulders softly as though filling the blank of affection she wishes were coming from me. "I was so in love with you, Stuart," she sighs, and her eyes drift back down to the pink wall-to-wall carpeting with pizza stains and splashed Pepsi. The violent sounds of the surveillance loop keep mercilessly repeating. I notice the girl behind the desk giving us a sideways glance, then return to the bright green glow of the computer screen. There is no escape. Becky Marie Thane lets her long arms fall to her sides in surrender, the blue bandana dangling from her right hand. I return the *National Geographic* to the glass table and then I do suddenly get a picture of that time, some fleeting memory of a morning facing a New York window with a bowl clenched between my naked knees, and I say, just to be saying something, "Your hair is even redder than I remember," which make her burst out laughing, suddenly happy that I haven't abandoned the game.

"It's not real," she says.

"What?" I say, thinking she's referring to something metaphysical.

"The color. Lady Clairol. Out of a bottle."

"Oh— Well, it looks great."

"Thanks."

"Very . . . festive."

"Festive?" She giggles and fluffs the back of her head like a movie star. Then she gets embarrassed again and twists herself from side to side.

"So, how old were we then?" I stumble on without really wanting to.

"We were kids," she says.

"Were we?"

"*I* was anyway. I know that much."

"Kids—yeah, I guess."

"How many do you have?" she asks and her green eyes come to meet mine and the little twinge of sadness I'd been feeling turns to an undertow.

"You mean children?" She nods and her eyes stay hooked to me.

"I've got a whole bunch," I say.

"How many?" she insists.

"Five. But not all with the same woman."

"That doesn't surprise me." She smiles.

"How about you?" I ask.

"Two. I have two girls."

"Two. That's great. Where are they?" I say.

"Here. Well, I mean—"

"That's right, you're from Indianapolis, aren't you?"

"Yes, I am. You remember that!" She smiles.

"I remember your dad calling, back then. When we were sitting on the bed eating that stuff."

"Wheat germ."

"Right. He called to tell you there was a riot going on in your front yard. So it *must* have been sixty-eight, wasn't it? That was when there was a riot every other day."

"Must've been."

"Martin Luther King and—"

"Right."

"Everything exploding. Detroit. L.A."

"The whole world on fire."

"Seemed like."

"Well." She pauses, fishing for something more. "I didn't mean to— I mean, I was so shocked when I walked through the door and saw you sitting here. I couldn't believe it. I knew it was you as soon as I saw you, but . . . I thought, I can't just walk on by and not say anything. You know—just go on up to my room and pretend it wasn't you. I had to come back down and say something. I mean— all this time."

"No, I'm glad you did. It's great to see you."

"What in the world are you doing here? In Indianapolis."

"Just passing through."

"Oh—"

"How about you? I mean, if you live here how come you're in a Holiday Inn?" Everything stops. She goes suddenly numb and her lips start to tremble. For some reason, the background sounds seem to have gone silent, unless it's a pause between the reels. The girl at the desk stares at us now, as though she suspects something illegal is going on.

"My husband—" she says, and halts on the words. "My husband disappeared a month and a half ago. He—just took off."

"Oh, no," I say.

"He took the girls."

"No—"

"He may have left the country." I find myself standing and making a feeble gesture toward comforting her but I'd rather be running out the door.

"Have you— I mean, do you have help?" My mouth has gone dry. "Police? Lawyers?"

"Yes, I've gone through all that."

"That's a pretty serious— I mean, that's considered kidnapping, isn't it?"

"It *is* kidnapping."

"Have you got any clues? I mean—"

"We've followed some credit card debits, you know, gas stations, restaurants, but it's all led to dead ends. Everything winds up in Florida and just stops."

"Florida?"

"He has some family down there."

"What about the girls? How old are they?"

"Twelve and sixteen. There's still some investigation going on at the house so that's why I can't stay there."

"Oh."

"I just took a room here for the time being. I'm kind of in limbo, I guess." She casts her arm out limply and the blue bandana flutters up like a distant flag of truce. Her eyes scan the two plasma screens as the screaming and the gunfire start up again. "I'm sorry," she says. "I didn't mean to lay all this on you. I just saw you sitting here when I came in and thought—"

"No, that's okay. I'm glad you— It's just great to see you again."

She laughs, then breaks down, but quickly recovers herself and turns her shoulder to me. I move to console her, but she turns her back completely and crosses her arms on her chest again. The desk clerk girl is heading straight for me across the lobby with her laminated name tag pinned to her breast and an apologetic face. "I'm sorry, sir," she says, "but they've just confirmed that room I was telling you about. That 'smoking' room with two beds."

"Oh," I say.

"Yeah, they just phoned in to confirm it. They're on their way. I'm sorry about that."

"That's okay."

"There's a Motel Six just down off Twenty-five. They usually might have a vacancy. If you want, I can call down there, see if they've got something."

"Would you mind doing that? I'd appreciate it very much."

"No problem. I'll let you know." She turns and heads back to her post. Becky seems to have pulled herself together now. Her arms drop, and she starts brushing off the front of her coat as though she's just discovered lint. She turns back to me with a smile and rubs her eyes with the back of her hand.

"Well, I'm so glad I ran into you, Stuart. You look the same as always." She steps toward me with her hand extended, which I find slightly ineffectual under the circumstances, but I go along with it. Her hand feels icy and slim and she slides it back out of my grip almost immediately. Then she gives me a little peck on the cheek, like a sister might. It all comes back to me now, the smell of her soft breath. "Bye," she says abruptly and walks away, disappearing down the hallway again.

If I had a gun right now, I'd shoot both the plasma TV screens and maybe the overstuffed sofa and then maybe I'd start in on the glass coffee table and the Caribbean vacation brochure and all the *Time* and *Newsweek* magazines with Men of the Year on the covers. Instead, I wander back over to the desk, where the girl with the laminated name is being surprisingly helpful. I get close enough to read the tag as she squashes the phone between her chin and her collarbone while scratching down a note. *Lashandra*, the tag says, and it has a little yellow happy face to go with it. "Lashandra," I say to her, not knowing exactly which syllable to emphasize. She squints at me and holds a blue-lacquered fingernail to her lips, as though she's about to land a luxury suite down at the Motel 6. I signal to her that I no longer want the room by drawing my index finger across my throat, then head for the revolving doors. Lashandra calls out to me in dismay, "Sir! Excuse me, sir!" I turn back to her. "Don't you want the room? I think I might have found you something."

"No, thanks, but I do appreciate your efforts. You're very kind."

"Oh, no problem at all, sir. Sorry it didn't work out."

"Lashandra, could I ask you a quick question?"

"Sure, sir. Anything at all."

"Don't you ever go crazy listening to that TV all night long? That—murder?"

"Oh, I don't even hear it anymore. You know—it's just always on." She smiles and I pass through the revolving doors. The pistol shots fade behind the glass.

Outside it's dark and snowing lightly, flakes floating through orange light. I completely forgot that I left the car running, and my yellow dog is clawing frantically at the windows, seeing me approach. I let her out the back. She slides across a patch of ice as she hits the asphalt. Her tail is wagging wildly in circles as though she's picked up the scent of quail in the dead of winter. She dashes off toward a little square of brown grass to take a leak. I follow her under the glow of the No Vacancy sign, which I guess I entirely missed when I stopped here. The temperature feels like it's dropped down into the low twenties by now and the flying snow is making my eyes tear up. The dog must be taking the longest piss on earth. She just squats there with one hind leg weirdly raised, staring straight at me as though I might run off without her. Steam rises behind her. The hollow moan of the highway makes me wonder if I've finally broken all connections without even really wanting to.

I pop my dog back in the car and slide into the driver's seat, which is now red hot since I also left the seat warmer on. I'm about to drop the gearshift down into drive when I look up through the snow and there she is—Becky Marie Thane—standing directly between the headlights, staring straight at me with a look not unlike my dog's. She's standing there shivering, without her coat, and the snow catches hold of her red hair and glows in the backlight, like a halo. Am I now having a religious experience?

She comes running up to the window as I roll it down, amazed. "I'm sorry," she says, "I just thought maybe you'd want to stay in my room since you can't— I mean, I have a couch and everything. A separate couch. It's a fold-out, you know—an alcove with a sink. Not a whole room exactly but I just thought it would save you a trip in this weather. I'm not trying to—you know—"

"Oh, thanks, Becky," I cut her off. "I really appreciate it but I ought to be getting on down the road."

"All right, that's fine. That's fine." She smiles. "I just thought I'd offer. I wasn't trying to—"

"No, thanks so much though. It was really great to see you again."

"Bye," she says sweetly, and gives me a little fluttering wave, then blows me a kiss as I drive off. I watch her in the rearview mirror as she darts back into the lobby, stomping the snow off her shoes at the entrance. I'm trying to think what movie this reminds me of. One of those corny black-and-white forties Air Force films with tearful good-byes as Jimmy Stewart flies off into the wild blue yonder. Why is everything I'm conjuring up in black-and-white?

The snow is really assaulting the windshield now, as I head for the Louisville junction, the dog turning tight circles in the back, then dropping down into a ball and tucking her nose into her tail; resigning herself to yet another hundred miles of black highway. I start drifting off into the past as the visibility gets dimmer and whiter. Maybe there's a correlation between external blindness and internal picturing. I can see the edge of the mattress now and our gray bowls side by side; our knees touching. These are some of the other things that go sailing through my head as I strain forward to keep the car between the lines: Leaving the desert on a clear day. Boarding the Greyhound. Getting off in Times Square. Huge poster of a pop group from England with Three Stooges haircuts. Blood bank with a sign in the window offering five dollars a pint. Black whores with red hair. Chet Baker standing in a doorway on Avenue C. Tompkins Square Park, with its giant dripping American elms. Cabbage and barley soup. Hearing Polish for the first time. Old World women in bandanas and overcoats. Cubans playing chess. Rumors of acid and TCP. Crowds gathered around a black limo, listening to a radio report of Kennedy's killing. Jungles burning with napalm. Caskets covered in American flags. Mules hauling Martin Luther King's coffin. Stanley Turrentine carrying his ax in a paper sack.

I'm turning around. I'm in the middle of a blizzard and I'm turning around. I come up on a giant tractor-trailer rig jackknifed in the ditch. No sign of a driver. I'm up over the median now with the hazard lights flashing, hoping nothing is roaring down on top of me from the opposite lanes. I'm driving blind. I'd get off to the shoulder but I can't tell where it is. Something is happening to my eyesight from the constant oncoming flow and swirl of snow. I feel as if I were suddenly falling through space and the wheels have somehow lost all contact with earth. I really am coming completely apart now, shaking, terrible shivers, gripping the wheel as if any second I could just go plunging off into the abyss and never be found.

Somehow I instinctively poke my way back through the gray to the looping exit, and limp back into the Holiday Inn parking lot. The family from Tupelo are unloading their huge crew-cab diesel in the whirling storm, sliding their coolers and luggage across the icy blacktop. I just sit there for a while, watching them through the wipers, my hazard lights still flashing, and my dog getting very nervous about what may lie ahead. Maybe I'll just spend the night in the car, I think. Wait it out. That would mean leaving the engine running so I wouldn't freeze to death. That would mean that the dog would be whining and turning in circles. I turn on my satellite radio for some possible clue. The angelic voice of Sam Cooke comes on. I can't take it. I turn it off, not wanting to provoke a total emotional breakdown. Can I just sit here all night like this? Engine running. Dog turning. Lights blinking. Snow falling. Am I going to park this car or just sit here forever? What will happen when the sun finally comes out and the snow stops and the ice melts and the whole landscape is transformed into spring and stuff is blooming and farmers are running their gigantic combines up and down the long rows? What will happen then? Will I still be sitting here like this with the car running? What will happen when they discover that someone is trying to live in his car in the Holiday Inn parking lot? I've got to get this car parked!

So I do and then one thing leads to another, and I'm heading back into the lobby, not really looking forward to encountering Lashandra again, not really looking forward to waiting in line behind the Tupelo hot-rod family, but there I am. Thank God the TV channel has changed. Now it's news with some distinguished-looking dude in a suit, parading back and forth in front of a huge electronic map of the whole United States, magically touching it and brushing it in different areas, causing it to light up red in the South, blue in the North, giving the impression that the whole damn country is some cartoon show, divided up like apple pie, and that no one actually lives here, trying to score a simple room at the Holiday Inn in the middle of a blizzard somewhere on the outskirts of Indianapolis.

The Tupelo family finally trundles off with all their gear

toward the "smoking" room I had once coveted. Lashandra's face is unsure what expression to make when she sees me pathetically standing there again. It's a cross between smiling politeness and sheer terror at what she must see in my eyes. "Lashandra, hi," I say meekly. She says nothing. "I was wondering if you could do me a favor, I— the storm is really bad out there. You wouldn't believe it."

"That's what they were saying," she says. "Those folks from Tupelo."

"It's unbelievable. Whiteout. I could barely see the hood in front of me."

"They've got it on the news," she says. "All the way down into New Orleans, I guess."

"Really? Well— I couldn't— I had to turn back around."

"I still haven't got any vacancy though," she says.

"No, I know. I know that. But what I was wondering is— I have an old friend here. That woman—you know, that woman I was talking to before? That tall skinny woman with the red hair?"

"Right," she says.

"I was wondering if you could give me her room number, because she offered to let me stay in her room and—"

"Well, we're not allowed to give out the names of guests, sir."

"No, I know. I mean— I know her name. Her name is Becky Marie Thane and and we used to live together in New York. Way back, I mean."

"Well, I still can't just give out the room number, sir. That's our policy."

"I understand that, but do you think I could call her, then, on the house phone? Would that be all right?"

"Sure. I can let you do that. Let me get you connected." She slides the house phone to her, looks up Becky's room number, punches it in, then hands me the receiver. I'm holding it to my ear, hoping Lashandra will stop staring at me and turn her back discreetly, but she stays right there, eyes boring into mine. Becky picks up.

"Hello," she says, and the simple innocence of her voice starts me weeping and I can't stop and Lashandra finally turns away.

These Recent Beheadings

These recent beheadings are just what we've always dreaded. We knew it was coming sooner or later and now it's here. Ancient gleaming steel coming down like a message from the heavens on our exposed white necks. The kind of separation that terrifies us the most—losing our heads. The absolute shock of sudden separation. The body here, the head over there. And the mind desperately darting between them, trying to pull them back together. How did this happen? From out of nowhere. Seemingly. Nobody saw it coming. Nobody could predict this. Not in 1957, anyway, when Chevy came out with that great fin on the Bel Air, and Little Richard was just hitting his stride.

Classic Embrace

They were having a conversation about Marlon Brando in *One-Eyed Jacks.* He remembers that much. He can see it in some motel room with a fire, off the coast of Santa Barbara; the Pacific crashing outside their window. He remembers her saying: "Remember how he lied to the beautiful señorita with the red hibiscus in her hair?"

"Oh, that's what it was—hibiscus?"

"Yes. That fancy red flower she wore just above her left ear."

"Oh," he must have said, "but what was the lie about? I don't remember him lying."

"Yes, don't you remember, he tells her there's something in her eye. Some little fleck of something. He makes that up and she believes him. She starts blinking just from him suggesting it. Then he unties the bandana around his neck and slides over close to her and starts gently poking at her eye with a corner of the bandana.

And, as he's doing this, he casually slips his arm around her waist and before you know it they're locked in a classic embrace."

"But that's not a lie, that's just plain old seduction," he remembers saying, and just as he'd said that he remembers something failing in his eyesight; colors dissolving, shapes disappearing, the foreground suddenly receding into flat smoky sheets.

"Is that when you first noticed you might be going blind?" she says.

"Yes, I think it must have been. But I do remember that flower."

"The hibiscus?" she whispers.

"Yes, I remember that flower hovering over her ear."

"Like a spotlight, wasn't it?" she says.

"Yes, but I don't remember him lying, to tell you the truth." They roll over toward the fire and he enters her from behind.

Alpine, Texas

(Highway 90)

I would come untracked, is what it was. At least, that's the way I see it. Now. In aftermath, so to speak. Disorient. For days it would come and go like that. Days and days. Wake up in some sheetrock room where the train shook the roof off. So close to the window you could reach out and lose your whole arm. Take your breath away. It did. Tucumcari. Kalispell. Abilene. Patriotic wallpaper. Blues and whites. Liberty Bells. Cracked plaster. Everything. Peeled right through to where you could see the old slats and newspaper insulation dating back to the late twenties. Those funny button-looking hats the gals all wore. Model Ts and pinafores. Headlines about the coming Crash. Was it a rendezvous or something? Some kind of secret meeting-up with someone? I wasn't sure. Lost track of the reason for being there. Days spent trying to track down license plates. That one with the orange Grand Canyon for instance. Perfect clue. She must've been an Arizona gal. Who could tell by now? The way I'd just be wandering around looking for hints. Sometimes the faint sound of a bird was enough to tip me off. I'd head out across the ancient zócalo at dusk, crossing the broad Avenida Dolores del Río, following this song into the darkest night. But mockingbirds can fool you for sure. That's their game. Confusion. Diversity. Magnolia melodies sweet enough to take you in completely. Total seduction. And they're free of guilt to boot. No qualms at all about breaking your heart in two and tossing you out there to the dogs. Those dogs. Those mean little dogs. California. Texas. Baton Rouge. Wide range of melody lines, if you follow my drift. Very little loyalty though. That's what I've found. Very little. Grackles, on the other hand, you can almost always count on. Very trustworthy bird for place and time. Wake up to a grackle and a wonderful certainty fills your aching bones. Calexico. Texarkana. One of those. Long-tailed screeching bravado in the face of another scorching sun. Brings all kinds of news. Breaking news, if you like. But losing track of people altogether—that's the worst. The feeling. The ache in the chest. Completely emptied out. No people. Some, just gone forever now. You can't help that. But the other ones. The ones still somewhere. Still somewhere else. What happened there? Where's the string? If there ever was one. You can't not believe in that. Still, some I must've just drove off. I admit. Must have. Why in the world would they want to stick around a burning bush? A flaming Chevy. Fire blowing out both my Anglo-Saxon ears. Fire blowing out my ass. Catastrophic. A devastating smoking heap. Some of the other ones just fled, I guess. Just ran off. Some came back but it was plain by then they'd never find in me what they were looking for. Plain by the look in their downcast eyes. Terrible disappointment that has no end. That I can see. No end in sight. And me still banging around these dusty streets searching for breakfast. At this hour. Slinking sideways between slat picnic tables, old bent ranchers, Open Road Stetsons; talking steers and heeling dogs, straight-up Christians praying over crispy bacon strips and runny eggs. You find a clean dry space on the plaid oilcloth across from two skinny Mexican kids so lost in love their hands are stuck with superglue. Black Aztec eyes turned inside out; blind to the nasty world, gorging on each other's mouths while their pancakes turn stone cold.

All that time I'm referring to now. Careening around. Must've been working on something or other. Must've done some kind of job. That's what it was. It dawns on me now. Down there in dusty Alpine waiting for a check. Guy's name was Roberts Clay. Not a woman at all. They said I couldn't miss him. Carried a big black hickory walking stick. And here it was three whole days and no show from this Mr. Clay. Down to my last good pair of SmartWool socks. Staggering through the watermelon trucks. Could a matchbox ever in this world hold my clothes?

Mission San Juan Capistrano

It's a weird shirt, this one. Makes me feel like a little boy again—
too small and tight and pink. It's a handmade shirt. My mother
made it and that's a sure tip-off to the kids in school that you
haven't got any money. I'm a little boy no longer but when I put
this shirt on that feeling revisits me. It's not the same shirt as back
then. I'd never be able to get that one on. But this one has haunting
similarities and casts the same spell over my upper torso. The chest
feels vulnerable and bony. My neck sticks up like a chicken. The
arms poke out. My entire being is up for grabs. I'm somewhere
between six and nine. An older woman is clutching my hand. A
linen handkerchief dangles from her wrist, tucked into her watch-
band. The coastal breeze blows her black lace skirt around my
shoulders. I'm sure it's my grandmother. I recognize her Iroquois
hands with the bulging veins. I have the same thumbs as her. We
were born on the same day in the sign of Scorpio. She showed me
once in the sky—how the tail reaches clear out across the entire
Mojave. The deadly tail. Pigeons are flapping all around our heads,
trying to land on our shoulders and arms. We're feeding them corn
out of paper cups. The Spanish fountain is trickling. Brass mission

bells chiming a mournful dirge. The war is certainly over, but where was it? Distant islands? Across the sea? I don't know my father at all. I've maybe seen him twice. Both times he was in a khaki uniform and smelled like bay rum. People pet me on the head as they pass by, like I'm a little animal. I'm entirely under the spell of affection. My whole body tingles from it; voices, movement, laughter, the smell of Pacific salt. Everything touches me in this way; straight through the skin. I *am* an animal. At night I sleep with my eyes wide open. Nothing escapes me. Not one sound. Bugs hitting the screen. My grandmother shuffling to the sink for her glass of water. The spotted dog moaning at the back door, wanting to get in; making the sound of loneliness.

It's a weird shirt—too small and tight. It sends me back to when I ran around in a completely different body and the unknown was much bigger.

Pity
the Poor
Mercenary

I cut his face off meticulously. That's all I have to say. Just doing my job. They told me they wanted the face as proof of the pudding. Trouble is it's not the same as skinning a walleye or a yearling buck. The human being is different. More curves and twists. The musculature, connecting tissues of the epidermis—not the same at all. Plus, all I had at my disposal was a Victorinox stainless steel jackknife with a four-inch blade. Sharp as a razor but nonetheless— had to force the idea of butchering out of my mind and just get on with the business at hand. There's never any use complaining. You just have to go ahead and get the work done and get on with it. I decided the best method of preservation was to dust the inside of the face with baby powder and salt, then roll the paper-thin skin into a loose roll. I bound the whole thing up with blue rubber bands, like the kind they use for holding broccoli and carrots together. I have to admit, the procedure was pretty much experimental since I'd never had to tackle this kind of thing before. Used to be they'd take you at your word. Why would you lie? You didn't take a target out, he'd come back to haunt you. That's for sure. No doubt about it. But this particular outfit claimed they needed concrete proof. Concrete.

Let me start again. Let me just start by saying, I fully expect to get paid for a job well done. That should be well understood right off the bat. Everyone does. No one goes blithely into something like this without expecting compensation—especially a job of this magnitude and scope. I mean, there have been others where you get half in advance and then the other half on delivery. And by "delivery" I don't mean bringing in a man's face, I mean just your good word that you left his head in a ditch by the side of the road or tossed it in a lake or something. And they'd for sure believe you. Why would you lie about something like that? Your reputation is on the line. And, back in the day, that's all you had to go on—your good word and your reputation. But now—these days—look at these jokers. No ethics of any kind. Outrageous— For them to suddenly renege and back out, denying any connection—trying to completely divorce themselves from any knowledge— I mean— Let me just say, I never would have volunteered for an assignment of this kind if there hadn't been a big score guaranteed on the back end. I mean, the skinning of a man's face— Are you kidding? If verification is what they were after, what's the matter with good, old-fashioned photography? The black-and-white Polaroid. I'm no Stieglitz but, hell, I can take a damn snapshot: "Before" and "After." I mean, look, when we took that creep out of Chad back in '95, that's all they needed back then. A plain old snapshot; "blip," he's sitting there stupid, staring into the lens with his arms bound back, obviously still in the land of the living and then—"blip," his eyes go black and there's a hole in the bridge of his nose big enough to jam a cigar—lights out. I got the fat paycheck on that one, believe you me. No questions asked. But this— It's beyond embarrassing.

Quanah, Texas

Dogen's Manuals
The Story of Ruffian
Machado's *Border of a Dream*
The Legacy of Conquest
Goodbye to a River
4 Plays by Tom Murphy
Dictionary of Spoken Spanish
Under the Volcano
Nineteen Elastic Poems

These are some of the indications of my current, scattered state. I'm looking at them point-blank.

Pea Ridge Battlefield, Arkansas

My second great-grandfather, Lemuel P. Dodge, had his left ear
blown off right here, in the battle of Pea Ridge, 1862. I have a picture of him, back home in my kitchen, sitting in profile, legs regally
crossed at the knees, dressed in his Confederate uniform. A thick
gauze bandage, bulging at the ear, lashed around his head. Both
hands gently rest in his lap atop an ornately engraved sword and
scabbard. His nose is a nose I recognize down through my father's
side. Uncles and cousins. His red beard and hair. His ice-blue eyes
like some Christian martyr. (The tintypes of the day may have
accentuated these features for the vanity of the sitter.) It's the
ghoulish white bandage that confuses the formality of the pose, as
though honor and raw violence have no real business sitting side
by side. "Six salvos of Federal artillery—eighteen rounds of rifled
solid shot smashed broadside into the massed rebel columns."
Horses exploded. Riders cut in half. Blood of the body. Pride of the
mind. The only sound right now in this ancient open field is a lone
mockingbird sitting on top of a yellow round bale. His tail twitches
with every change in the melody line.

San Juan Bautista

(Highway 152)

Some things do come back: we stopped in San Juan Bautista and tried to call Luis Valdez from a pay phone (long before the days of cells). I barely knew him but this was his town and we were passing through so— A woman with a heavy accent answers, says he's in Oaxaca but try later, he might be back later. She says this as though he's just down at the Quik Stop buying cigarettes. Later? I say. What do you mean, back later? Oaxaca's a long way off isn't it? Oaxaca's in Mexico, we're in northern California. She hangs up as though I'm some kind of prankster. John now is talking nonstop and has been for the last two hours. Part of the reason I wanted to stop and make this call was just to get out of the car and away from his ranting, but here he is, still carrying on. Now it's about Ansel Adams and his light meter techniques. As though I gave a shit. Just running off at the mouth about apertures and stops, regardless of the immediate situation; the fact that we've stopped the car now and we're out in the light of day in this bright town and something new might be just around the corner. He just keeps right on yakking about Ansel Adams. I, myself, was never a huge Ansel

Adams fan if you want to know the truth. Too precious about the landscape for my taste. I mean I respect the landscape as much as the next guy, don't get me wrong, but I'm not going down on my hands and knees to it. I'm more into faces—people; Robert Frank, Douglas Kent Hall, guys like that, but John, he can't stop gushing. I think he's on speed again is what I think. In fact I'm sure of it. Unmistakable behavior patterns: dry mouth, smacking his lips all the time, twitching his neck around as though trying to adjust something; hunching his shoulders up and scratching both fore-arms at the same time. These are dead giveaways, if you ask me. He promised me and Dennis he wouldn't bring any of the shit along but I'm sure that's what it is. What else could it be? He's got a hidden stash somewhere in the Chevy. He's done this before. No honor. Another telltale sign is the constant switching of subjects with little or no regard for what's just come before or what might follow. As though he doesn't even need a listener. Just willy-nilly random whacked-out associations, shifting blithely in midstream like we're a couple of tourists walking through his inner landscape. Just as an example; now he's talking about lying—that's his subject for the moment: the Art of Lying, he calls it; the myriad forms of self-deception on the liar's part. A liar who doesn't even realize he's lying as opposed to one who does. Ultimately, he says, there's really no difference between the Intentional Liar and the Unintentional one since neither of them is capable of seeing the entire context in which their lying takes place. And then he says this: "They are blind to the repercussions of their fabrications." He actually says that. I stop dead in my tracks and look into his twitching eyes. I have the urge to kick him in the ass but I don't want to start this trip off on a sour note.

We stumble into a quaint little café, pretending to be ordinary polite citizens off on a little road trip; as though it's the forties or something, back when whole families just piled into automobiles and rambled down the road for the sheer enjoyment of shifting scenery. We sit down at a table draped in a red plaid oilcloth with salt and pepper shakers in the shapes of a rooster and hen. There's a big plate-glass window looking out over the old Spanish plaza. Everything seems quiet and peaceful even though John picks up the salt and pepper shakers and starts humping the hen with the rooster. Before we can even order coffee Dennis starts up on something and I can suddenly see that he's in on this speed thing with John. Same symptoms but slightly more subtle. He starts in on a dream he's been having where there's this big-ass guy in shorts swinging from the ceiling of an old courthouse by his knees and then crashing to the tiled floor and just lying there, pretending to be dead. Just deliberately crashing like that. I'm not used to men telling me about their dreams. There's something suspect about that for some reason. Women, I don't mind doing that, but men is a different story. So long as he doesn't start interpreting this dream, bringing in astrology and runic symbols and trying to draw parallels to his waking state, I can go along with it. I manage to order bacon and eggs with chorizo sausage and corn tortillas on the side between the gaps in Dennis's musings. Actually, the only reason I'm tolerating this dream-recall of his is because he once related to me the details of his father's suicide and I keep waiting for another spellbinding tale to come out of him like that one but so far it's not happening. His father owned a hardware store up in Oregon, and apparently, one night after closing hours, he managed to rig up an ingenious pulley device with nylon cord and fishing line fastened to the triggers of a Browning over and under, enabling him to place his forehead directly in front of the black barrels and pull both triggers at once. There was little left of his father's face. Dennis was ten at the time and remembers the community up there shunning him as though he were suddenly akin to the insane. Now John pops up again in one of the long pauses of Dennis's dream. He says he suddenly realizes why he's always liked crime novels so much. I was unaware he had any passion for the genre at all. He says it's because he's always identified with the isolated nature of the detective as a central character. The outsider looking in. He says that just before we entered this café here for instance, he had that same kind of feeling—that "outsider" feeling and his reaction was to immediately take on the persona of the Detective; turning his collar up, stuffing both hands deep in his pockets, keeping his eyes low to the ground while maintaining an acute awareness of the café's interior. (I just assumed it was more goofy speed behavior.) Having adopted this new facade gave him confidence, he says, to enter the café and order a cup of coffee. He says he finds it much easier to play a role than to be himself since he has no idea who in the world he actually is. He was purchased on the black market back in the forties for six thousand dollars cash at the age of one from a Jersey City adoption agency. The Jewish couple who bought him said they picked him out for his little shock of black hair, dark eyes, and certain Hebraic features which they thought might eventually cause him to be mistaken for their own flesh and blood. As he matured, however, these characteristics became more and more exaggerated, taking on definite simian qualities his surrogate parents could never have predicted. His nose broadened and flattened out something like Rocky Marciano's. His lips became full and pouty and he developed the habit of never quite closing them. His eyes took on the deep black sheen of an Italian Gypsy and his hair hung in shaggy ringlets with no bounce to them at all. On top of all this his general attitude toward the outside world veered far afield from his parents' expectations. He was entirely without ambition of any kind. As early as twelve years old he would sit for hours on park benches and stare at the pigeons. He had no desire even to feed them. His only dream was to fall madly in love with a Spanish redhead and live with her forever in some remote village, taking occasional side trips by himself but always returning to her bed. He's managed to achieve this and claims to be completely satisfied with his current situation. I have no reason to disbelieve him.

Dennis now comes up with this sudden revelation that this has to be the town where Alfred Hitchcock shot *Vertigo*. He remembers the tower. We're looking directly at it out the plate-glass window. He remembers Jimmy Stewart's climb up the winding stairs and the woman falling—or was it the man? Maybe that's why I'm having these falling dreams, he says. Not me falling but someone else—like, you know, that guy hanging from the courthouse ceiling—deliberately crashing to the floor like that. I'll bet that's what it is, he says.

What's what it is, I ask him as I unscrew the Texas Pete.

Vertigo! The movie. You remember that movie, don't you? Jimmy Stewart and Eva Marie Saint.

No, it was Grace Kelly, John pipes up.

No, it wasn't Grace Kelly, Grace Kelly was in *The Birds,* Dennis says.

That was Tippi Hedren, I interject over the eggs.

Oh, right, Dennis says. She was the mother of Farrah Fawcett, right?

Farrah Fawcett?

Farrah Fawcett is not the daughter of Tippi Hedren, John says. I've been away from the cinema for some time, I admit, but I'm almost positive that Farrah Fawcett is not the daughter of Tippi Hedren. She's the mother of somebody else very famous but it escapes me right now.

I thought it was Farrah Fawcett, says Dennis.

No, you're mistaken.

Well, who is it then? says Dennis. Who's she the mother of?

I'm not sure. It'll come to me, says John.

Why don't you guys go take a walk around the plaza while I finish my breakfast, I suggest.

All right, good idea, says John and off they go out the door, the two of them. Just like that. It's like they're totally suggestible. All you have to do is suggest something and they go along with it. Like if you said to them, why don't you both go climb that Alfred Hitchcock tower out there and push each other off, they'd probably go along with that too. They've got to be stoned out of their minds.

Both of them. I think maybe Dennis is on some of that Purple Owsley acid or maybe just mushrooms. I saw him plucking something colorful out of the cow shit by the side of the road when we stopped to take a leak. I can tell by the way he's walking—all slow and disoriented, carefully observing the smallest dumb thing. Like stopping dead in his tracks to watch a paper cup go blowing across the bandstand. I can see them both now out the plate-glass window as I chew on my tortilla. How did I get to be the observer in this bunch? The outsider of the outsiders. Now they're both squinting against the sun, shading their eyes with their hands and walking slightly hunched over with their collars up, like they've just been released from a very dark place into the light of day. Like two ex-convicts actually; two guys who have just recently spent some very serious time in stow and don't have a clue how to behave in society anymore. My arrogance is beginning to take its toll on my stomach but I'm having a hard time switching to tolerance with these two. I don't know why I end up judging them all the time. I thought we were just going to roll on down the road and let everything happen. Like the days of old.

Brain Fever

There was definitely some inbreeding going on way back there between the Bateses and the Fiskes; the Dodges and the Smiths. You can see it clearly in the 1400s then trailing back deep into the Dark Ages; the Ferrers and the Lyons, Norman horsemen; the Walkers too ("those white barbarians," as Benjamin Franklin was wont to call them). They were fucking each other's cousins. It's plain to see in the family tree. They were all mixing it up. In Thoroughbred parlance the polite term for it is "linebreeding." You'd be hard-pressed to find a racehorse these days without at least one ancestor repeated in the first four generations. The popular superstition about this in human practice is that it leads to domestic violence, bad teeth, and insanity. Now, the polite term for "insanity," back in the day, was "brain fever." It shows up again and again in the annals of my ancestry: "succumbed to brain fever, 1636, in transit to America aboard the schooner *Peregrine.* Fell into a feverish spell and wandered off into the woodlands, believed captured by the Narragansett. Burned at the stake for furies of the mind, conversing with devils in most unintelligible tongues."

It's enough to make you wonder.

Tops

Things like these—lost fragments, almost: At sixteen, working for Tops Chemicals, loading buckets of chlorine in green flatbed trucks; did I, for instance, connect the raging sting in my eyes at night and the jaundiced tone my hands had turned with swimming pool hygiene and bikini moms? I doubt it. I had no idea either, for instance, that the acres of exotic flowers next door carried a name like *bird of paradise*. Who dreamed that one up? And how these cut flowers brought top dollar in L.A. after running all that way by train at night through Santana wind in pitch-black boxcars to be opened up to the morning dew by Mexican vendors then sold for the shady patios of the super-rich Wrigleys and Richfields. I was an innocent kid, as they say; skinny as a whip. Dogs came out to meet me. Grown women smiled and waved from porches. I had no clue they kept right on watching through their kitchen windows as I cut down across the orange groves and hopped the tracks of the Union Pacific.

Things like these just come floating in these days. Uninvited.

Thor's Day

(Highway 81 North, Staunton, Virginia)

What was that all about last time, anyway?

What last time?

In the Cracker Barrel. Denton. When you broke down for no apparent reason.

I can't remember.

You don't remember suddenly bursting into tears after you ordered those blueberry pancakes? You don't remember that?

No— No, I *do* remember but I can't remember why.

Totally embarrassing. Everyone staring. The whole place went silent.

I remember. I remember now.

Well, you should remember. It was only three days ago.

Day out of Days

Is that all?

That's all.

Seems longer.

That's all it was.

How long have we been on the road, anyway?

Too long. I can't stand this. I really can't.

It's not all that bad.

It's bad.

Do you think we should go our separate ways?

Ha. What would you do without me?

I'd be all right.

What would you do?

I'd be fine.

You'd be fine. You can't even order pancakes without blubbering into your napkin. What's become of you, anyway? You've fallen completely apart.

I'll be fine.

Stop saying that! What has happened to you? Has somebody died or something? Somebody you're not telling me about? Some dog, maybe?

Nobody's died. Nobody recently, anyway.

Then what is it? What in the world could be so tragic?

I don't know. It just comes over me.

What does?

A black cloud.

Oh, stop. I'm not falling for your poetics. Just try to control yourself while we're having lunch. I want to eat in peace.

. . . . .

Do you want to sit by the window?

Yes. I like to look out on all the parked cars.

How's this?

Good.

Which side of the table do you want?

I want to be able to see all the parked cars.

Day out of Days

Fine. I'll sit over here, then.

Don't you want to sit next to me? Side by side, like we used to?

No. I want to sit over here. Across from you. So I can keep an eye on you.

In case I break down again, you mean?

Exactly.

You don't trust me.

It's not a question of trust.

We always used to sit side by side.

That's not entirely true.

Back in Roswell, we used to.

That was a long, long time ago.

Seems like yesterday.

Your sense of time is out of whack.

We always sat side by side in Roswell so we could hold hands and touch each other's thighs.

Will you please stop with this! Now, what do you want to order?

What do they have?

The same thing they always have.

Do they have those pancakes? Those blueberry pancakes?

You're not ordering those again.

Why not?

Because they make you break down and weep for some mysterious reason you don't understand.

It wasn't the pancakes.

What was it then?

I told you, I don't know.

There's got to be a reason.

There is. I just don't know what it is.

How can that be? How can that possibly be?

. . . . .

Is today Thursday?

Yes. I think it is.

Then they must have chicken and rice. That's what it says: "Thursday Special—Chicken and Rice."

Is that what you're having?

I don't know.

Well, make up your mind. The waitress is heading over here.

Do you know where "Thursday" comes from?

What?

"Thursday." The word, the day. Do you know where it comes from?

I have no idea.

Druids.

Is that a fact?

Yes. "Thor's Day"; the day of thunder. The Thunder God.

Thor? I thought he was Norwegian or something. Viking. He wasn't a Druid, was he?

No. He was a god.

And they worshipped him? The Druids?

They worshipped everything.

That can't be right.

They worshipped the oak.

The oak?

Yes.

The tree? The oak.

Yes.

And why was that?

It was the tree most struck by lightning.

Fine. Are you having the chicken and rice or what?

It was the tree Thor chose to strike and set on fire.

Where in the world is the waitress?

It was the tree the Druids climbed in white robes and cut the mistletoe from with golden daggers.

I can't believe they leave people just sitting here like this.

They thought the mistletoe was a message from Thor.

I'm going to find the waitress.

No! Don't go!

I'll be right back.

Please, don't go!

Oh, stop it. I'm coming right back.

Please!

Oh, my God! What'd I just tell you about this? This is exactly what I was talking about. Now you're trembling.

Just don't go.

Let go of my wrist!

Please!

Let go! You're hurting me!

I'm sorry.

You've punctured the skin. Look at that!

I'm sorry.

I'm going out to the car.

What? Why?

I'll wait for you in the car.

I thought you wanted to have lunch.

Not anymore. I'm not hungry.

Please. Come on. I want to have lunch.

Let me just tell you something—and the only reason I haven't come out with this before is that I didn't think you could handle it. I was afraid you'd break down again, but now I see that it's just impossible to keep this going—this—especially after what you've just done to my wrist. I want you to know that I think we've . . . come to the end of our days together. And that's the short truth of it. We've come to the end. What else is there to say?

What am I supposed to do now?

You said you'd be fine. That's what you said: "I'll be fine."

I was just saying that.

I can't go on with this anymore. I really can't. Look what you've done to my skin.

I'm sorry.

It's like an animal's been chewing on it. Look at that! Look at this blood! It's all over the place.

I'll get some ice.

No! You've done enough damage already.

Here, take this napkin. Wrap it around your wrist.

No!

Oh, here comes the waitress. Finally. Here she comes. Over here!

Day out of Days

I'll meet you in the car.

Over here, miss! We'd like to order!

I'm going out to the car.

No, the waitress is coming. Look! Here she comes.

I'm going out to the car.

No!

· · · · · ·

I'm sorry, sir, but I didn't see you sitting over here in the corner. All tucked away.

That's all right.

Would you like to hear about our specials today?

No.

So, you know what you want then?

Is it too late to order the blueberry pancakes?

Cracker Barrel Men's Room

(Highway 90 West)

I understand there was a man who got trapped inside a Cracker Barrel men's room, once. (I've heard the story three or four times now in various convenience stores and gas stations just outside of Butte, so there must be some germ of truth to it.) He was trying to take a dump in peace in one of those oversize stalls for the handicapped (even though he wasn't). He liked the extra space around him, the aluminum handrail, the hooks to hang his hat and coat. It must have been after closing hours, I guess, because the night manager had mistakenly locked him up in there and had also left the sound system on and, evidently, Shania Twain songs played all night long in an endless loop. Over and over, that's all he heard was Shania Twain. She sang songs of vengeance and good riddance, infidelity of all stripes, callous treatment at the hands of drunken cowboys, maudlin ballads of deprived youth, the general inability of men to see into her hidden charms; songs where she refused to be a slave anymore to the whims of men, like for instance making toast, doing the dishes, washing clothes, frying an egg, shopping for groceries. She wasn't buying into any of that stuff. Then she had songs full of praise for her mother; prayers to her baby sister, her great-aunt, her sister-in-law, her sister's sister-in-law. She praised God for making her a woman. She praised Jesus for her spectacular body and her luscious red mane falling down to her luscious ass. The man became desperate to escape the Cracker Barrel men's room. He tried to dismantle the door hinges with his trusty Swiss Army Knife. He tried pounding the walls. He tried screaming his head off but there was nobody there. No dishwasher, no waiter, no cashier, no janitor, no night manager, no one but Shania Twain, over and over and over and over again. There was no escape from the onslaught. The man collapsed to the tile floor in a heap of resignation and tried to fall asleep but sleep wouldn't come. Shania's voice taunted and tortured him. She clawed at his ears with her long silver talons. He hauled himself up off the floor and turned all the water faucets on full blast. He punched all the hand-dry blowers. He flushed every toilet but nothing would drown out the piercing voice. He could still hear it pealing through the background somewhere; whining away in mawkish misery. He tried climbing up on top of the toilet stall and unscrewing the speaker but he stripped all the screwheads with his trusty Swiss Army Knife and fell backwards to the floor, impaling himself with the open blade. He writhed in pain and managed to extract the knife from his left thigh but blood gushed freely into the overflowing water of the sinks and steam was rising like out of some primordial stew. He dragged himself through the darkening red mess of it, back toward the door, moaning like some butchered stockyard animal. He kicked with his one good leg and flailed his hands and screamed one last time but nobody answered; nobody but Shania Twain in her endless refrain. Then he surrendered completely and did something he'd never done in his entire life. He prayed. He prayed to Jesus to stop the bleeding. He prayed to God for a little peace and quiet. He prayed someone might find him before he drowned in his own fluids. Then a miraculous thing happened (and this has been verified by at least two eyewitness accounts—window washers at the very scene); the men's room door swung slowly open and there she was—Shania herself, towering before him in her spectacular body, her spectacular red hair, her spectacular lips, her spectacular tits. She was singing her head off. She was singing like there was no tomorrow. She didn't seem to notice the man on the floor, bleeding to death. In fact she stood right on his chest in her green satin stiletto high heels and kept right on singing. She seemed to be focused on something in the far, far distance but it was hard to tell through the steam.

Face

The other big question I have, and believe me I have lots of them, is this— A face is a face only so long as it remains attached to the muscles and blood supply of the body; and that body and blood supply are attached to the person. Once you separate the face from the body and lay it out flat on a Formica counter like that it's not the same thing anymore at all. It's not a face. It's not a person. It's a pelt, or something. A remnant. A trophy. I don't know. Wouldn't you agree? It's certainly not recognizable as part of a living being anymore. Not identifiable. So who came up with this shit? This might have worked back in the frontier days when we were tracking down Apaches in Arizona, but this is the twenty-first century, for Christ's sake.

Costello

I made the great mistake of returning to my hometown after not being anywhere near the place for over forty-five years. Why do we do these things when we know full well they're going to bring nothing but sorrow and grief? Some morbid curiosity in the place itself, I guess. The plain streets. Trees grown bigger. Porches where you used to toss the morning paper off the handlebars of an orange Schwinn. Why would anyone volunteer to take a stroll through their distant past other than to torture some memory of a long-lost counterpart?

I had come to the end of it quickly; actually vomiting in the front yard at the sight of our old adobe stuccoed house where there once was a red canvas awning, now replaced with a taxidermy sign below the head of a pronghorn antelope. It wasn't the thought of slaughtered wildlife that got me, it was slaughtered youth.

I had lost track of where I'd left the car and found myself staggering down the shoulder of Highway 66, which had acquired a new name I couldn't pronounce. Something rhyming with Santana Wind in bastard Spanish. It made me dizzy trying to repeat it in my head. Traffic blew by in waves of anonymous urgency, as though everyone were hurrying off toward a great final festival in the desert. I was the only one on foot. I stopped and checked in all directions for any other fellow pedestrians; nothing moved but cars and traffic lights. I spotted the only familiar structure from my childhood—an old gray donut shop called Krispy Glaze where I used to hang out after school just to behold the spanking-clean blonde girls in ponytails and petticoats. I couldn't believe this place was still standing. As I entered the glass door a miniature cowbell clattered above my head, awakening sensations of adolescent yearning. Same bell, same sensations. I ordered black coffee, a glazed donut, and a glass of water to wash away the rancid taste of puke. I sat in a corner, just like I used to. Same corner. Same vantage point. It was a perspective I've long maintained: back to the wall with a clear vision of everything moving in front of me. Poker-style. The place was empty except for a man about my age wearing a blue serge suit and black tie, sitting in a booth in the opposing corner. I hadn't noticed him when I first came in and would have picked a more oblique location had I seen him sitting there. I prefer not to be stared at when I'm furtively staring at others. I make no bones about my obsession with observation. I enjoy making notes. Jotting things down. The way he snapped his *Racing Form* with little flicks of the wrists and licked the tip of his pencil. Who even uses a pencil anymore? Besides, my little notebook gave me the needed disguise of being preoccupied with my own thoughts, casting no suspicion that I might be closely observing his every move. There is a subtle art to the sneaking of glances. Timing is everything. To look as though all your attention is completely absorbed in the subject of your notebook when, in fact, you are lurking; waiting for the moment he picks up his coffee cup, takes a chomp out of the donut then unabashedly sucks the sticky sugar off his fingers while continuing to scan the morning workouts. These are the ripe spans of time where you seize the opportunity to look deeply into the essence of a man; see the source of his greed without his having the slightest clue. Still, you have to be constantly alert; wary of not getting caught by his quick glance. In the flash of an eye he might become aware that you are a witness and begin subtly altering his every manifestation; playing out the illusion that he is in total control of his character or worse—he might become hostile and paranoid. I've seen it happen. People hate to be seen. They hate the sensation of eyes on them; being looked at for what they are and not what they imagine themselves to be. Very few people can handle the blatant stare except children under five. This has been my experience anyway.

Often, in the midst of caution, coaching yourself to be careful, the danger presents itself, in spades. This is exactly what happened. He caught me staring right at him. I had become so fascinated by the surface and contours of his deeply pockmarked face that I had completely let my guard down. He glared at me in disgust, snapped the paper viciously, then propped it up so as to conceal his entire head. My first impulse was to run. Just abandon my half-eaten Krispy Glaze and skulk off like a beaten dog. But I was afraid this would only raise his suspicions. I still had no clue where I'd parked the car and I wasn't about to go wandering off down the side of the road and get shot in the back by some madman with a pock-marked face in a blue serge suit. I had felt something intrinsically violent about him from the start. He had a smell. Even across the empty space I could catch it. Effusive use of cheap aftershave and cologne that would probably make your eyes water if you got too close. And the suit and black tie— Who wore that kind of outfit anymore except lowlife hustlers and hired thugs? Punk chumps who sold snapshots of some businessman's wife fucking the check-out boy in the parking lot. I could feel him stabbing me from a dis-tance with his eyes. I remained, chin on my chest, riveted to the notebook as though studying the secrets of Osiris or something but I knew I'd really kindled his paranoia. His agitation was palpa-ble and became more insistent. This guy could be anybody, I thought. What if he's part of some cartel. Some ring of evil. You never know. Out here on the edge of nowhere. This is exactly the kind of territory they like to operate in. Semirural. All kinds of agricultural pesticides available. Fertilizer. Methamphetamine. Bombs. He could be anyone. The *Racing Form* should have tipped me off right away. Pomona wasn't that far down the road. I used to work there in high school, walking "hots." I'd seen, firsthand, all the dregs of the earth, hanging off the rail, slinking down the shed rows. Snakes of men who'd sooner slit your throat than give you the time of day. He could be one of those. Or worse. What if he thinks I'm a witness—not "witness" in the sense I was using it before but a witness to some heinous crime he'd committed? I'm getting way too carried away, I thought to myself. I should have followed my instincts and never come back here. This place has never held any luck for me. What was I thinking?

Now the worst began to happen. He slammed his paper down in front of him, pressed both fists into the "past performances," and stood straight up. He brushed donut crumbs off the lapels of his suit jacket then walked right over to me. My eyes never lifted from the notebook although I was acutely aware of his every move. My heart remained oddly still. He came to an abrupt stop right in front of me and the waves of cologne caused me to catch my breath. "Am I supposed to *know* you or something?" he said, extending the word *know* as though it might have deep connotations. I tried my best to look up at him, calmly bewildered.

"Excuse me?" I said.

"You been looking at me."

"Oh, I'm sorry."

"I thought maybe you recognized me from somewhere."

"No—no, I was just—noticing your *Racing Form.*"

"What about it?" he said flatly.

"Oh, nothing. I was just—wondering where you picked it up. I've been trying to find one."

"Down at Dewey's. Liquor store."

"Oh, great. I'll run down there and get one, thanks."

"You know Dewey's? Right across from the Oasis?"

"I'll find it," I said.

"You sure I don't know you from somewhere?"

"I don't think so, no."

"Track, maybe?"

"No. I'm not from around here."

"Where you from?"

"Uh—back East."

"East?"

"Yeah. Vermont."

"Oh, yeah. Maple syrup, huh?"

"Yeah."

"Cold."

"It can be."

"What're you doing out here?"

"Oh, just—you know. Knocking around."

"Not much to it, is there?"

"Well—"

"Never has been. Lost souls wandering in the desert. That's what I call it. Lost souls."

I chuckled as though in on some local joke. He made a slight clicking sound between his teeth like he was asking a horse to pick up into a gallop. I wondered if I'd ever get rid of him. "I swear I recognize your face from somewhere," he continued. "You ever played in the movies?"

"What?" I said, genuinely shocked. "No."

"You look just like that guy— What's his name?"

"What guy's that?"

"That guy in the pictures. What's his name. You could be his double."

"Is that right?" I said.

"Yeah. You know who I'm talking about?"

"No."

"Anybody ever tell you you look just like him?"

"Yeah. Sometimes."

"Thought you said you didn't know who I was talking about?"

"Well—no—right. I mean—"

"This guy used to live right here in this town, ya know? Fact I went to high school with him."

"What guy?"

"This guy I'm talking about. The one in the movies. Went off and changed his name. That's how come I can't think of it. Got some Hollywood handle now. Used to be called Billy Rice. That's what I knew him as anyway."

"Billy Rice," I muttered as though memory failed me.

"That's right. Ever hear of him?"

"No. I never did."

"Well, you look just like him. Spitting image."

"I'll be darned."

"Lotsa guys I've known changed their name. Different reasons though. Anonymity. That's the key to it."

"Right."

"Mind if I sit down?" he said, and there was nothing I could do to stop him. He crouched right across the Formica table from me on the edge of the seat, as though any second he might make a lunge for my throat. He folded his hands neatly in front of him, stitching his thick fingers together. I could feel his eyes boring into me but I couldn't look him in the face. I kept all my focus on his hands, hoping this whole encounter would pass as quickly as it had started. I'd never seen such a collection of rings like that on a grown male. Every finger glimmered. Even the thumb on his left hand was entwined by a silver serpent with tiny ruby eyes. This thumb kept rubbing slowly over the knuckle of the opposing one in a smooth hypnotic rhythm as though preparing for a strike.

"Yeah, it was a funny thing. So long ago. Billy. We used to hang out."

"No kidding?" I said.

"There he was, up there on the big screen. Outa the blue. I could've shit my pants."

"Must've been a surprise."

"It was. You remind me a lot of him. Older, but then it was forty-some years ago."

"That's a good long while."

"It is. Lotsa water under that bridge. We'd get drunker'n ten Apaches back then. Wild. Course I think he was part something. Some tribe or other. Had those shifty eyes. Couldn't hold a thimbleful of whiskey without trying to rape everything in town."

"Is that right?"

"Oh, he was a loose cannon, that one. No fear, in some areas. Course there's only a cunt hair separating crazy from courage. We used to run all kinds of scams, back then. Stole cars and drove 'em down to Mexico. Dismantle the bastards and sell all the parts. Made tons. Buy Benzedrine down there by the sackful. Right across the counter. No ID, driver's license, or nothing. Back then you got away with anything. Wide open. Whores. Pills. Slaves. You name it."

"Slaves?"

"Kids. You hire 'em off the street to do a job. You know what I'm saying?"

"Oh, yeah—"

"Need somebody's dick cut off, they'd do it. Cheap too. Five, ten bucks. Desperate."

"Man—"

"You think I'm kidding? Billy could tell you. Fact I could probably blackmail his ass with half the stuff we pulled back then. If I knew where to find the prick. Big-shot movie star. New name and all. Fancy women. Corvettes. Got a whole collection of vintage Sting Rays in some garage in Malibu, I heard. Same car we used to boost. Same exact model. Big 454 engine. Overhead cams. Sell like hotcakes down there in Tijuana. Used to have one fandango of a time, I'm telling you. Chicks. Hellholes you wouldn't believe. You made damn sure they knew you were carrying when you walked in or they'd cut you up like fish bait. Stuff we saw— Girls fucking dogs and donkeys, right on stage. Right under bright lights. Talcum powder blowing around in clouds. High-heeled men who could fool you into a hand job if you weren't careful. Got in free too. Just drinks and tips was all. And us only sixteen years old and couldn't speak a lick of Spanish. Then we'd come flying back across that border, usually with some greaser pachuco on our tail and head straight for the American liquor store. Stand up on some parked car and wave the finger at him, across the Rio. Those were the days. You talk about some good times."

He came suddenly to a stop and stared out the window toward the highway as though looking for a lost connective thread. His hands shifted and now the right thumb wound up on top of the left and picked up the same methodical rubbing. His voice shifted and dropped an octave: "Never in a million years would've thought we'd go off in such different directions. Just fate, I guess. I mean him just falling into that Hollywood craphole like that. Famous and all. Face on the cover of every magazine. You know— And me—well—me just sitting here staring out the window."

"Yeah," I said, trying to soothe the moment. "You never know how things are going to turn out."

"You got that right," he said, and stood up in the same abrupt manner, brushing imaginary crumbs off his jacket just to be doing something. He stared down at his tie and adjusted it, cinching the knot up a notch. "Well, it was nice visiting with you. Sorry for the interruption. Looks like you were busy with your notes there."

"Yeah—no—just jotting stuff down. Just a habit. You know—"

"Well— You ought to try getting ahold of that guy's movies. That Billy Rice guy—whatever his name is now. You look just like him."

"Yeah. I will. I'll do that."

"You can get the DVDs right down there at Dewey's when you go for your *Form*. I've seen 'em on the rack. He must be in a dozen of 'em."

"I will," I said, and then he suddenly extended his hand across the table at me.

"Name's Costello. Eddie Costello. Sounds Italian but it's actually Irish. County Cork." He attempted a faint smile as I took his hand and felt the silver snake bite down on top of my knuckles. It was quick and lethal and then released.

"Pete—Pete Davis," the name just came out of me from somewhere.

"That's Welsh, isn't it?"

"What?" I said and now my heart clicked in. I looked straight into his eyes for the first time and saw what I'd deeply dreaded. His terrible hooded eyes in their scarred sockets. The light had gone completely out of them.

"Davis," he repeated. "That's Welsh."

"I guess—yeah."

"Well, good luck at the track if you're going out there. Buncha damn dog-food claimers in there today. Couldn't beat a fat man uphill."

"Thanks," I said as he headed back to his corner, picked up the folded form, then turned and tipped it in my direction like men in the forties used to do with their hats. When he went out the glass door the little cowbell made the same metallic clammer and the same sickening sensations jumped up in my skin. Dimmer this time. I watched him walk across the parking lot toward a blue Ford Galaxie sedan and just as he reached for the keys in his pocket he made a little squirting spit between his front teeth. It darted out in a thin brown jet. I remember how he always used to do that just before we'd jump a car and roar off toward the border. Just before we got into all that trouble.

Time Line

Aug. 28—Police find 11 headless bodies outside Phoenix. All corpses were handcuffed. One was nude and showed significant signs of torture.

Sept. 12—Police find 24 bodies, 15 of them decapitated and many with signs of torture, in a field west of Laredo. Most have gunshots to the head.

Oct. 1—Eight bodies with gunshots to the head, two decapitated, are dumped next to an elementary school in El Paso. A note attached with staples to the tongue of one head reads: "Here are your people, *cabrón*. Come get them!"

Dec. 21—The heads of 8 soldiers and a former chief of police are found in a vacant lot next to a Kmart in Tucson. A note says: "For each one of mine you kill, I'll kill 10 soldiers."

Shame

When I was a kid and carried eucalyptus in my pocket and my T-shirt smelled like the dogs that ran with me, every time I killed an animal, back then, with a bow, a gun, or a knife I'd bring it right into the kitchen and throw it down on the floor. To show off, I guess. Why else? To be seen as a hunter. Dripping blood. The raw smell. A snake. Rabbit. Dove. Beheaded squirrel. My sisters ran. Every time. My mother quietly cried and picked the dead bird up, hanging limp across her weathered hand. I can't remember feeling shame. I can't remember feeling at all. Maybe I'd already grown dead by then. I went right back out, looking for game.

Esmeralda and the
Flipping Hammer

(Highway 152, *continued*)

I'm getting very distracted by an extremely cute Mexican waitress in here, named Esmeralda, I find out. She's wearing this little pink frilly apron over her tight jeans and she keeps my coffee cup full without me having to ask. She has a smile like the break of day and an "onion ass," as old cowboy Jones used to say: "Just makes you want to break down and weep." In fact, she reminds me of that little Mexican girl that Kerouac took up with in *On the Road*. That was my favorite part of the whole book; where he meets her on the bus from L.A. and sits down next to her and they wind up living with her parents and her entire family somewhere in the San Joaquin, probably not too far from this place right here. They're migrant workers up from the Sonora Desert all living in this little one-room shack, speaking no English, and Jack seems ecstatically happy for a while, working alongside her in the blazing hot fields, cutting lettuce and balling her silently in the dark night of the shack so as not to awaken the little family and maybe get his throat cut by the father. It's nice to think of Kerouac happy like that for a time, after he got so totally wasted toward the end; living with his old mom somewhere down in Florida and blowing his belly out with wine. I don't know about Kerouac, though, as a man; as a person. Of course you probably never do about anyone who's done something like write an important book that a lot of people say changed their lives. I don't know about that one either—actually having a piece of writing change your life. I doubt it. Maybe for a spell. A day or two, but your whole life? I find that hard to believe. But, anyhow, there was this guy I ran into who knew Kerouac and also had the good luck to know Woody Guthrie at the same time and had taken a lot of photographs of Woody during the last days of his life. You know, those stark black-and-white portraits of Woody staring stoically into the camera with that goofy high hair-cut he had which I think must have inspired Lyle Lovett. So, when this guy met Kerouac he told him he thought his writing was great and how much it reminded him of Woody's songs—how the songs and *On the Road* seemed to make a harmony about American lost-ness. But, according to this guy, Kerouac didn't take the compari-son as a compliment at all. In fact he became indignant and belligerent (probably blind drunk) and starts yelling at this guy: "Woody Guthrie's just a folksinger! I'm a poet like Rimbaud and Verlaine! I'm a fucking poet!" That made me think different about Jack for a while, but I don't know, I wasn't there. You can't depend too much on hearsay but I did run into Cassady once in a garage up on Haight Street in the sixties and he was exactly the way Ker-ouac portrayed him; crazy as a box of squirrels, flipping a claw hammer over and over and catching it every time by the handle. Never said word one; just kept flipping that hammer and chewing on his lower lip. Talk about speed. I was impressed. This little wait-ress is driving me crazy.

John and Dennis come stumbling back into the café like Abbott and Costello just as I'm paying the check and trying to score the waitress's number. They just come bumbling right over and butt in like there's nothing at all happening here between me and the girl. They don't even notice I'm getting close to promoting something. That's how out to lunch they've become on their smorgasbord of drugs. Who knows what combination they've been popping now. So much for heightened awareness and all that Timothy Leary bull. Dennis has this big shit-eating grin on his face and holds up some kind of San Juan Bautista arm patch he's bought in a gift shop, with bright orange California poppies embroidered on a sky-blue background. Some tourist bauble he's picked up in a marijuana daze. He dangles it in front of Esmeralda, grinning away, as though she's never seen anything so remarkable as this before. She's probably born and raised right here and he's carrying on like it's something wonderful and unique. Esmeralda turns and stares at me with this blank expression like: "What's the problem with your friend?" Now, realizing that my chances with the enchanting Esmeralda have quickly gone up in smoke, I leave her a mighty tip and we all exit into the stinging light of day.

Tet Offensive

It was the height of the Tet Offensive and they were fleeing west across the bleak Saskatchewan plains in a rented Karmann Ghia convertible. He remembers now, although he can't for the life of him remember what they were fleeing from. He can picture the two of them clearly; top down to the hot prairie wind, extremely young and the paranoid girl so pregnant she'd completely lost control of her bladder. She was barely sixteen and all she read on the drive out there were *Conan the Barbarian* and *The Green Hornet* while he chain-smoked Luckys and kept the hammer down on the Ghia. Every ten miles or so something in the comics would strike her as unbearably funny and she'd break into hysterical laughter and piss all over the bucket seat. Then she'd stack blankets, pillows, and old comic books under herself to sop things up, which elevated her way above the frame of the windshield, and her red hair lashed back so violently it seemed as though her head might get ripped right off and go tumbling down the highway. Every moment, in those days, had the potential for total annihilation.

Mean Green

As soon as they saw the dead man's face tacked to the back of the motel room door, they started whooping it up. I couldn't believe it. Laughing and pointing right at it. All that time and trouble and there they were, hysterical, as though it were some sort of child's attempt at inventing a toy. Humiliating, to say the least. "You don't actually expect to get compensated for something like this, do you?" That's what they told me. Right to my face. "Look at this— You can't even recognize it as the same man." That's exactly what I'd been trying to explain to them all along and now they were throwing it back at me, as though it were *their* idea. I told them that if you skin a man's face off, chances are it might go through all kinds of changes: shrinkage, disintegration around the edges, distortions of the mouth and eyeholes; even color—the skin tone—might be altered. For instance, a yellow man might easily become black or vice versa. You can never tell. But no, they didn't want to hear about it, back then. All they were het up about was eliminating the target. Making him go away. Immediately, if not sooner. So I obliged them. Now they were trying to back out of the agreement altogether. I flat told them they had no idea who they were dealing with and if they weren't very careful, some of their other little "projects" might start turning up mysteriously. Little remnants of appendages thrown randomly off the shoulder of Interstate 35, for instance. Or some piece of something from that grisly incident in Arkansas. You never know. All these little items might just suddenly jump up and bite them in the ass if they weren't careful. Next morning, cash was under the door in a sealed manila envelope. No name, no nothing. Just pure sweet mean-green.

Poolside Musings
in Sunny L.A.

In Cold Blood has seen a lot of mileage lately. Are they now replay-
ing old Robert Blake movies because he's on trial for killing his
wife and doing chicken imitations in court for the cameras? Why
don't we just bring back public lynchings and be done with it?

These tiny birds—sparrows I guess you call them—keep flit-
ting up on my table here, looking for crumbs. I have no crumbs
and if I had them I wouldn't allow wild birds to feed on them. I'm
not in favor of turning wild things into pets. Spoiled birds. We
don't have birds anything like these back home, as you know. All
our birds back home have some size and respect for human temper. How did fear and respect become synonymous? Whenever
there's a murder here, the suspect always says, "Maybe now they'll
show a little respect."

Seminole, Texas

bales and bales
of cotton
big as boxcars
flapping gray plastic sheeting
gangs and gangs
of crows
Christian radio
tungsten filaments
donuts and Texaco
pink donuts
and Texaco

the Road is not a Movie
no, it's not
no, it's not

Las Vegas, New Mexico

It's crisp December and the high mountain air has that sweet familiar scent of pine. Strings of tiny Christmas lights have just snapped on in the old Las Vegas Plaza, outlining the massive, leafless cottonwoods. Crows swoop down into the empty bandstand. I don't know what they could be looking for. One sits on the bronze plaque commemorating Stephen Watts Kearny's speech in August of 1846 when he climbed atop a pueblo here and addressed the entire plaza of bewildered Mexican citizens, some of whom had never seen a white man and had no notion of anywhere called "The United States of America": "I have come amongst you by the orders of my government, to take possession of your country, and extend over it the laws of the United States." After a long list of reasons why this idea should be appealing, not the least of which was offering better policing than the Mexican government could pro-vide against the savage raids of the Navajo, he capped the whole thing off with this blunt threat: "He who . . . is found in arms against me, I will hang."

From my second-story window of the historic hotel where the likes of Buffalo Bill and Teddy Roosevelt had laid their heads and dreamed their dreams, the plaza is completely empty now and silent. Only the crows strutting in snow. My cell phone glows green on the little round table beside the bed. Downstairs there's a loud man in the lobby bar. I've encountered him before and I avoid the bar now because of him. His name is Lorenzo. That's the way he introduces himself. "Lorenzo." No handshake, just the name. There's good reason to believe that Lorenzo has had his mind shat-tered by methamphetamine and various other destructive pow-ders. When he smiles at you it has an intrinsically malicious bent as though slitting your throat would be as simple as starting a car. Like some dogs, you don't want to catch his eye.

Parked directly in front of the old hotel is a giant-wheeled pickup truck that looks like one of those Tonka Toys except it has a dead mountain lion strapped with black bungees across the hood. Its mouth and yellow eyes are wide open. There's very little blood. Inside the cab of the truck two crossbred coonhounds are barking savagely and slashing at the window glass as though it might be their own reflections that have triggered their fury. Two fiddle players (I don't know where they've come from; everything just seems to appear) are playing in a big open brick room at the back of the hotel. No furniture, no plants, just a big empty room. They play in the old Appalachian Mountain style with fiddles braced against their hip bones and laid flat so the bows work at about waist level, giving them an odd detachment. They seem to have no interest in an audience and that's good because there isn't one. People (tourists?) stroll through the lobby and peek into the empty brick room then stroll on. I don't know if the hotel has hired these fiddle players or what. Now Lorenzo the Madman is suddenly screaming from the bar. He's screaming about football; something he's just witnessed on TV. A referee deserves to die. A huge athletic man on the bar stool next to Lorenzo is the owner of the pickup parked outside. He's a professional lion hunter, hired by the government to keep them thinned out and appease the surrounding ranchers. The lion hunter has a Mohican haircut and a turquoise earring. He's married to the plump bartender who speaks with a thick Australian accent and has a flamboyant way of drafting a Guinness. The lion hunter is in agreement with Lorenzo about the offending referee, ratcheting up Lorenzo's impotent violence. The willowy cocktail waitress is making every effort to be courteous and efficient as she weaves her way through the mayhem. Lorenzo screams and drools. She pretends that everything is absolutely normal. She has such innocent country eyes, a Mormon ponytail that bounces. I don't know where she's come from or how she arrived in this little corner of Hell but she won't last long. She keeps coming over to my table and asking me if everything's all right, as though I might be able to reassure her that the world is not coming to an end. "Yes," I tell her. "Everything's fine. It's just history running its course." She smiles sweetly and flees.

Nauvoo, Illinois

Site of the Mormon exodus to Utah. Seventy thousand of them crossed the wide Mississippi here in 1846, fleeing the rabid mob. The righteous drove them out. One testimony on the side of a building in block letters: a woman who hangs all her straight-backed chairs on the wall, sweeps out her plain board house, closes up all the shutters, puts the broom back in its proper place, locks up the front door, and says good-bye forever to her blessed home-place. She turns west to face a sea of salt.

Little People

The European missionary sat hunkered down in a squatting position with the Huron tribesmen in a great circle around the bonfire. It was a posture he was unused to and instinctively felt put him at a disadvantage insofar as persuading the Indians into his point of view. Nevertheless, he bravely presented the notion that he was not one but two. When the warriors heard this they broke into wild laughter and started throwing sticks and dirt into the fire, which created a strange mixture of terror and resentment in the missionary's chest. When the laughter subsided he pressed on with his contention. He patiently explained to the savages that this corporeal body they saw sitting before them was only an exterior shell and that inside him resided a smaller invisible body that, one day, would fly away to live in a heavenly domain. The Huron all chuckled and nodded to themselves as they knocked the ashes from their stone pipes into the crackling fire. The missionary felt deeply misunderstood and was about to get up and return to his tent in a huff when an old man next to him held him in place by the shoulder. He explained to the missionary that all the warriors and shamans present in the circle were well aware of these two bodies and that they also had "little people" residing inside them deep within the chest and that they too flew away at death. The missionary became excited at this new news and felt reassured that he and the tribesmen were now on the same path. With renewed zeal he asked the old man where his people thought these little interior beings traveled off to. The Huron all laughed again and the old man pointed to the crown of a massive ancient cedar nearby that flashed in silhouette from the firelight. He told the missionary these "little people" entered the very top of that tree and descended into its trunk and branches, where they lived in eternity, and that was why he could not cut it down to make siding for his little chapel in the wilderness.

They say, these days, standing out on the rim of the Grand Canyon, the brightest lights in the night sky are not the stars in the heavens but the glow from casino neon in Las Vegas—one hundred and seventy-five miles away.

Lost Art of Wandering

(Highway 152, *continued*)

I try calling Luis again from the yellow pay phone. I'm yearning for some variation on the company I'm keeping but he's still not there. A different woman from the first but with just as strong an accent tells me he's down in Chihuahua now and won't be back for at least a week. I tell her I thought it was Oaxaca where he was last and she says she doesn't keep track of him that closely, he moves around a lot; then she hangs up on me just like the first woman did. These two must be something to behold.

There's music and singing coming from the mission chapel so we head over there. We're just leaves in the wind. We pass a very Teutonic-looking tourist in a neck brace and a fringed Davy Crockett jacket who's trying to figure out his Kodak Instamatic. John stops and helps him with it. John is very good with cameras, I must admit. He loves fiddling with them, the lenses and straps and stuff. He's a natural with cameras. The tourist guy is overjoyed that a total American stranger has stopped and gone out of his way to help him. He's very impressed with John. I think he must be German or Dutch or gay or something. Very strong accent and he's wearing those weird European sandals that buckle up the ankle and look like they're made out of phony leather. And on top of that he's wearing them over a pair of thick army-green wool socks. It's funny but I've found you can actually pinpoint where people come from by the sandals they're wearing. Like Mexicans, for instance, prefer those huaraches with black rubber soles made out of old tires. Pakistanis generally like those flimsy jobs with the leather loop around the big toe. I've gotten pretty good at identifying nationalities that way. Stereotyping. Of course, you're bound to make a mistake now and then. John looks like he's finally solved the problem with the man's Kodak and the man is extremely grateful, trying to give John money and bowing and scraping, hauling out twenties and tens but it seems like he doesn't quite know the difference in the denominations so he's just holding out fistfuls of money but John won't take it. Deep down, John is basically a very honorable guy. He has what you might call true moral fiber although it beats me where he came up with it. He's done a lot of reading and he once attended a Krishnamurti lecture. I think it was actually a series of lectures out in Big Sur somewhere. I'm not sure. Now Dennis is telling John that he should accept the money from the German guy; we could use it for gas and cigarettes but John still won't take it. So now the German guy tries giving the money to Dennis but Dennis says he wasn't the one who fixed the camera. The German keeps insisting, shaking the money up and down in both fists, so finally Dennis pockets forty bucks of it and hands the rest back to him. Then John starts yelling at Dennis to give the forty bucks back so Dennis pulls it out and tries handing it back but now the German refuses to take it. He throws his hands up and steps back as though saying, "A deal's a deal." Now John really goes ballistic and starts screaming at the German, "Take your money back you stupid fucking Kraut! What's the matter with you?" People are turning to stare at us now from across the plaza. Peaceful people on vacation. "Do you think Americans are all on the take? Is that it? Huh? Do you think we're incapable of generosity and goodwill? Or is it your historical racial guilt that's causing you to treat me like some lowlife beggar?" The German keeps smiling and nodding and thanking John then turns and walks away, just like that, leaving Dennis with the forty bucks still clenched in his outstretched hand. John snatches up the money and goes running after the guy, yelling insults all the while, but the man keeps right on walking, ignoring John and taking snapshots of the mission and the tower where Alfred Hitchcock shot *Vertigo*. Finally, John just throws the money at the German's sweaty back, yelling more insults about the Third Reich, then stomps back over breathlessly to where we are. I've never seen him in such a state. He's trembling now and spitting at the ground. Quite a little crowd has gathered to watch this altercation, but now, seeing that it's not going to develop into physical violence, they disperse. Dennis says we should go and pick up the money that John's thrown away. The German's making no move to retrieve it and we could really use it for the miles up ahead. It's ridiculous to leave good money lying in the dirt, he says to John. John's eyes are glazed over as though he's about to throw up. It's the principle of the thing, John pants, as we watch two little Mexican kids in shorts and bare feet go running across the plaza and snatch up the forty bucks. Dennis yells at them but they just run off as fast as little ponies. Dennis isn't about to chase them. He's in terrible shape. We're all in terrible shape. I don't know how we got this way. We used to be young and vigorous; now we're standing here like a bunch of desperate winos or something. How does this happen?

We wander our way into the little Mission chapel where all the singing is coming from. Kids are running up and down the aisles laughing and giggling while the old people stand singing "Glory, glory, hallelujah" in Spanish. We try to sing along but our Spanish isn't that hot and religious hymns never turned me on anyway. Nobody seems to mind that we've just walked in and joined their ceremony even though we're strange-looking gringos with blood-shot eyes. Maybe they've just grown numb to the presence of tourists in their town. Or maybe they possess true Christian spirit. Doesn't seem like they care one way or the other. Nobody's trying to control the kids either. They just keep running wild up and down the aisles. The priest doesn't care. It's great. The women all have these snow white embroidered pañuelos on their heads. The men hold their straw Western hats in front of them with both hands, heads bowed and eyes open; eyes wandering around as they sing almost mechanically. It's beautiful, though, the singing. Even though I'm not normally moved by religious hymns. There's a beauty to the whole simple event of it. A few of the older men have their eyes tightly shut and their lips are moving silently; speaking to the Lord, speaking very personally. No sound, while the singing surrounds them. Then the singing stops and the people all sit back down in the wooden pews. It strikes me that this moment and this repetition has been going on for centuries; praying, singing, sit-ting, praying, on and on like that. And here we are with nothing to hang our hats on. The kids settle down and group up with their parents and families. The priest steps up to the altar in front of a huge golden crucifix. It looks like it was dipped in caramel like a candy apple from the county fair, the whole agonized Christ and the cross and everything, as though the real Christ were suffocated under layers of goo like those ancient victims from Vesuvius. The priest adjusts the gooseneck microphone at the podium, obviously uncomfortable with technology and even slightly irritated by it. The mike makes a growling sound. The kids giggle. They remain right in the moment. No one reprimands them. Then the priest has a little coughing attack right into the microphone. He stifles it and apologizes. The kids think this is hilarious. Even some of the elders find this funny. The priest looks embarrassed and adjusts his stiff collar. Dennis leans over to me and says in a hoarse whisper: I wish I'd have been raised Catholic, don't you? I love all this stuff. I have no idea what he means and I'm not going to ask. We leave the little chapel just as the priest gears up for his sermon.

Now we find ourselves ambling down to the rodeo grounds, having nothing better to do. Whatever happened to our jobs? Didn't we once all have jobs? John was working in a Mexican delicatessen making up breakfast burritos with white rubber gloves on. Dennis was working as a dogcatcher. And I had something connected with the Highway Department, mowing the medians. What happened? Did we all just up and walk away from being responsible adults? It's a mystery to me. We still have a lot of miles to cover down to Los Olivos but there's no deadline. There's nothing like having no deadline. John and Dennis are much better at it than I am. They seem to be able to totally accept the mutable nature of things whereas I'm always looking for an objective of some kind, somewhere down the road. John has actually become an artist at doing nothing; totally satisfied with just being here and not worrying about the next thing coming up or stewing about something in the past you can't do anything about anyway. The Lost Art of Wandering, he calls it. He's put a title on it so as not to confuse it with plain old indolence. That's what his stepfather always accused him of, he says—laziness. He's told me that since he was about thirteen years old he's had the distinct sensation that he's been living in his own past and observing it, as though he were already dead. Kind of like that narrator guy in *Our Town*. I admire that about John even though I don't quite get it. He comes up with some profound shit sometimes.

We encounter a strange glass display booth in front of the rodeo stands with an earthquake seismograph inside it. The whole thing is sitting on a kind of Greek pedestal as though it were commemorating something historical. There's a handwritten sign on the glass that reads: OUT OF ORDER. We're in earthquake country. I forget that sometimes. I forget lots of things these days then sud-denly something will come back, some thought or something, almost like a picture in my head that gives me this whole feeling about pieces of the past. A past I never lived in. Like, for instance, that book *Two Years Before the Mast* by Richard Henry Dana— what a book that was. This aristocratic New England Yankee guy who sets off on a sojourn around the Horn in a three-masted schooner clear up the entire coast of early California and writes this detailed diary at a time when Spain and Mexico owned the whole damn thing. The Hide and Tallow Days they called it where they'd toss dried-out cowhides off the cliffs down to the beach from the mission near San Luis Obispo to the schooners waiting in the cove below. Stiff cowhides sailing hundreds of feet through the blue Pacific air so they wouldn't have to carry them down the steep incline where even burros couldn't make it. Things like that just break my heart.

Duke of Earl

Writing to his London superiors in 1771 regarding the Appalachian border and the impossibility of keeping Scotch-Irish settlers east of an imaginary line running down the spine of the mountains; the very last English governor of Virginia, the Earl of Dunmore, wrote:

"My Lord I have learnt from experience that the established Authority of any government in America and the policy of the Government at home, are both insufficient to restrain the Americans; and that they do and will remove as their avidity and restlessness incite them. They acquire no attachment to Place: But wandering about seems engrafted in their Nature: and it is a weakness incident to it, that they Should forever immagine the Lands further off are Still better than those upon which they are already settled. . . . they do not conceive that Government has any right to forbid their taking possession of a Vast tract of Country, either uninhabited, or which serves only as a Shelter to a few scattered Tribes of Indians. These notions, My Lord, I beg it may be understood, I by no means pretend to Justify. I only think it my duty to State matters as they really are."

Taos

Squawking magpie. Brilliant light. The past gone past. The past gone by. Kit Carson's grave site on the back side of town. Forgotten, by the kid's slide. Ragged chain link. Old Kit at fifty-nine. My passport keeps falling to the ground like a dead blue leaf. Slipping away. This brilliant sight. Golden shaking poplar. Great cottonwoods. Shaking in the sun. Trembling like the tremblers of old. Navajo. Feathered helmets. Puma skulls. This brilliant light of day. Indifferent to sunken graves. Molding stone. Weathered away where you can't even read the names. Metal plaque honoring the hero. The scout. The man who crisscrossed the country by mule. Whose dying words were in Spanish. Graffiti knife slashes across Kit's neck. As though he'd feel a thing. As though a vengeance could still hold power in this bright corner of buried bones and no feeling; absolutely still except for the twirling golden leaves.

My passport keeps falling to the ground. Maybe it's trying to tell me something.

Wyoming

(Highway 80 East)

The long haul from Rock Springs to Grand Island, Nebraska, starts out bleak. After two runny eggs and processed ham I hit the road by 7:00. It's hovering at around nineteen degrees; light freezing snow and piss-poor visibility. Eighteen-wheelers jackknifed all along the high ridges between Rawlins and Laramie. Tow trucks blinking down into the black ravines. Through wisping fog, things loom up at you with chains and hooks and cranes; everyone inching along, afraid to drop off into the wide abyss. Just barely tap the brakes and the whole rear end slides out from underneath you. I'm trying to keep two tires on the shoulder in the chatter strip at about five mph hoping the ice will get dislodged between the treads. Only radio station is a preacher ranting from Paul—something about the body as a tent; "this tent in which we groan." Same preacher segues into a declaration that, for him, 1961 was the absolute turning point where the whole wide world went sour. I don't know why he landed on that particular year—1961—the very year I first hit the road, but he insists this is the date of our modern dissolution. He has a long list of social indicators beginning with soaring population then family disintegration, moral relaxation, sexual promiscuity, dangerous drugs, the usual litany. But then he counters it with the imperious question: "What must the righteous do?" As though there were an obvious antidote which we all seem to be deliberately ignoring. If we could only turn our backs on this degeneration and strike out for high ground, we could somehow turn the whole thing around. It seems more political than religious. "What must the righteous do?" An "Onward, Christian Soldiers" kind of appeal. I've lost track of the centerline. Snow boring down into the windshield so fast the wipers can't keep up. Your heart starts to pump a little faster under these conditions; not knowing what might suddenly emerge. Not knowing if the whole world could just drop out from underneath you and there you are at the bottom of crushed steel and spinning wheels. What *must* the righteous do?

Buffalo Trace

I am stuck now in a town of backyards. This is not a dream. There are no houses to speak of so it can't really be called a town, certainly not "Our Town" or downtown Milwaukee or something identifiable like that. There is no center; no Main Street but the people stroll along as though they had somewhere to go; some destination or another—purposefully but without any urgency like they would in a Big City, hustling and bustling just because everyone else is, as though caught up in a fever they can't escape. More like a walk in the park; meandering but not really wandering so much; not really lost like me who seems to be the only one the least bit bewildered. And it's not as though I don't recognize certain signs; not signs like stop signs or signals because there are none. No advertising of any kind. Very much like the East Berlin of old, before the wall came down. (Hard to believe I once drove through there in a gray Ford Anglia, reading Brecht quotes below the barbed wire while they wheeled a mirror back and forth under the axles, searching for something I might be bringing across illegally.) But now I do recognize certain backyards from years and years ago; certain fallen fences, single-track dog paths worn down through the cooch grass connecting immense vacant lots where vague footprints of very large warehouses once existed and there must have been a great traffic of oxen teams and black mules coming and going, throngs if you will; blacksmith hammers ringing down the broad avenues. And beyond these lots, fields stretching right out to the highway with volunteer oats and blue timothy undulating in the prairie breeze. And the highway itself, now broken up with tall yellow weeds and potholes deep enough to kill a Ford of any kind and, what's even more revealing, is that now the dead highway seems to be returning to the ancient buffalo trace beneath it where someone must have tried to copy the migrations of vast herds that once blackened the landscape. Maybe they felt the buffalo knew where they were going even if they themselves didn't have a clue.

"Our dwelling is but a wandering, and our abiding is but a fleeting, and in a word our home is nowhere."

—*Separatist leader at Plymouth, 1620*

Original Sin

Now, I've heard this story before, bandied around, about "original sin." The Adam and Eve deal. The snake in the garden and all that shit. She bites the apple. He goes along with it. They take the plunge and fuck their brains out. The spare rib syndrome. The pains of childbirth. They have to start hiding their genitals with fig leaves. The guilt and remorse. I've heard that one. My grandmother read me that story while I balanced on her knee. I've heard about the Pilgrim Fathers and how we descend directly down from the *Mayflower* folks and the Plymouth Colony and those same Puritans tramping around on Cape Cod in their funny hats, digging up Narragansett burial mounds and stealing their ceremonial corn when they're supposed to be doing God's work. I've also heard how Jesus died on the cross for our sins and rose again from the dead. The Holy Ghost. The roll away the stone. How we need to constantly beat ourselves up for being such miserable thankless Godless creatures, crawling around on our bellies like a bunch of reptiles. But how in the world are you supposed to make a living? That's my question. How are you supposed to scrape two nickels together? I've tried everything: busboy, waiter, fence painter, wrangler; raking up chicken bones from fancy picnics. Nothing pays as

Day out of Days

good as shooting some fool in the head and moving on down the
line. Believe me, nothing. With a check like that I can lose myself
down in the Yucatán for months on end. Live like a damn poten-
tate. Brown beauties all around me. Tequila up the ass. Float on my
back in the green Caribbean. Are you kidding? One less tyrant in
the world is the way I look at it. Jesus might have died for somebody's sins but they sure as hell weren't mine.

The Comanche were known to plunder English Bibles in their raids on westering wagon trains; ripping out the onionskin pages and stuffing them into buffalo hide war shields emblazoned with blue horses, red hawks, and running dogs.

Choirboy Once

I can hardly believe I was a choirboy once. There it is. Evidence. Picture of me in the fifties. Back there in the fifties. Innocent. Or so it seemed. Snapshot: Ike and Spot. Frigidaire gleaming. Picture of me in black robes. Puritan floppy white collar. Butch haircut. Waxed and perky. Look at that. Crooked squinting smile, unsure what it's projecting exactly. The smile. Pinched lips. What's it trying to say? What's it hiding? I can't remember being there, to tell the truth. But something must have been. Some other one. Not me now. This me now. Not this one here. Some other. Watching. Staring out. Watching very closely. The proceedings. Rituals. Nothing escaped me, if that's what you think. Wafers and wine. Flesh and blood of our Lord. Cannibal congregation. Swarming sex. Submerged. Fever. Bulging behinds. Crotches rock hard. Christ on a stick. Blood of the feet. Dripping nails. Mothers of friends. Sisters.

Girls' rear ends. Sex. Chicas. Lipstick so thick it crumbled right off into their steaming black laps. Fingernails of the Virgin Mary. Raw smell of pussy. Right through the cotton. Singing. Chants. Incantations to the one and only. The Holy of Holies. The Triple Threat. Voices praying. Knees buckled. Going down on the velvet. Rustling thighs. Silken calves. Going down on Jesus. Crucified. Bleeding through and through. Then gathering back up. Struggling to the surface. Gasping for air. Back up to the Lord. For mercy or what? Echoes off the stone walls. The droning voice. Sermon. Protestant. Certain. The whole effort of it. The jaw. The teeth. The distance from life. The great distance. Outside. From here to there. Out there. Where the hot cars sit parked. Waiting. Steaming black top. Outside in the heat. Hot air. Just waiting to roar off to anywhere but here. Tonopah. Wichita. Anywhere but right here.

Cat in a Barn at Night

If you go to shoot a cat in a barn late at night and you want it quick and sudden so as not to wake the children; whatever you do don't use a pistol. You'll never get it done. The son-bitch will run howling all up and down the rafters with a slug right through his skull and you'll never find him in the dark. I'm telling you. Don't even think about using a handgun. If you can manage to catch the bastard, drop him in a burlap oat sack and tie it shut with baling wire. Don't forget to use mulehide gloves and long sleeves or he'll slash your white skinny ass to ribbons. Hang the sack to a stout beam and back off no more than five foot. Shoot the sack point-blank with a full choke twelve-gauge loaded with steel goose pellets and have a whole boxful on hand in case the bag keeps twitching. I'm telling you. Don't even think about using a pistol.

Philip, South Dakota

(Highway 73)

He lost his head completely. I don't know what set him off. Just started firing and firing and firing. In a circle. Gas pumps exploded. People fell. People ran for cover. I don't know what set him off, tell the truth. They closed the Cenex—the feed store—Dairy Queen. All those little shops around there. They just folded up and went away after that. It's like a ghost town now. I'll take you down later if you want to see it. Shocking. Completely deserted. Weeds. Broken windows. Nobody. I don't know what set him off. I really don't.

Nephophobia

(Veterans Highway)

Fear of clouds? Why? Out of the whole panopoly of phobias, why that? There was a name for it. He looked it up. A title. Something reassuring about it being named. Someone's had it before him. He thought. It's already in the world. He thought. Someone else is or has been already possessed by clouds. Succumbed. In this way. "Nephophobia"—that was it. Possibly Greek? Clouds. Antiquity. Ticking away. All across the naked Alleghenies that day. Driving the twisted 64. The "Veterans Highway." There they were. Extremely close. Hanging above the mountains. Piled up faces. Clouds misshapen. Faces in the heavens. Horrible. Bloated cheeks like those old cherub angel paintings. Medieval. Caravaggio. Gouged-out eyes. Gigantic demons from on high. This was going to be a difficult trip. Just getting across. Just getting over to Stonewall Jackson's old stronghold where he bled to death from "friendly fire." (It's not such a modern term.) Could he make it? There was no stopping now. No pulling over. He tried his best to not look up. Keep his mind on the road. What was left of it. Hug the rumble strip. But there they were—sucking his attention. Seducing him up into looking. And now they'd change—the eyes, the cheeks. Like flesh sloughing away. The heads sliding off. Joining other heads. A whole family. None of them looking related. But then they'd melt; one into the other. Becoming others. Ancestors, maybe. Could he make it across? Could he make it through this? Just stay between the lines. Grip the damn wheel and stay between the lines. It's not that big a deal.

Victorville, California

(Highway 15)

Queens Motel, with a dull green plaster brontosaurus, all chipped and peeling from the desert sun, standing tall on its hind legs in front of a huge black satellite dish facing the Roy Rogers Mountains. I hadn't realized they'd actually named some mountains after Roy. I'd never heard of the Roy Rogers Mountains and I grew up here. I grew up with Roy. He was one of the first television cowboy heroes I can remember watching. I watched Roy in the flesh too, riding Trigger down Colorado Boulevard in the Rose Parade alongside Dale Evans. I had no idea he got some mountains named after him. That must have happened long after I left. I wonder who decides that, anyway. Who decides to give mountains a name—or streets? They must do that by committee or something. I know a guy down in Texas who got his dad's name put on a freeway outside Dallas because his dad owned the asphalt company that poured the road. Then there was a little side street in New York City called Thelonious Monk Place. It might still be there. I thought that was cool. Somebody must have really had to lobby for that one. And then, of course, they're always renaming stuff too. Taking the old name down and putting a new one up. That happens all the time. Dictators like to do that. Have you noticed that? Totalitarian tyrants. You never know how long a name is going to last from one regime to the other. Like, for instance, the Roy Rogers Mountains could have a Chinese name in fifty years. You never know. Roy could be long forgotten by then if he isn't already.

Victorville, California

Monk might last a little longer than Roy but you never know. Of
course you can't really compare East Coast idolatry to West Coast
and it's probably not fair to allegorize fifties cowboy heroes with
iconoclastic Jazz Legends but there you go. In fact fairness isn't
even part of the issue. I don't know why I brought it up. Maybe
there won't even be any mountains left at all, let alone streets.
Nothing left to name. *I'm* not going to be around, that's for sure.
Still, I wouldn't mind seeing some of these names changed but it's
not going to be in my lifetime. The Richard Nixon Library, for
instance. Bob Hope Airport. Ronald Reagan Drive. How about
having a Joaquin Murrieta Boulevard? He got his head cut off and
paraded around the streets of Los Angeles on a stick and they don't
name shit after him.

Elko, Nevada

(Thunderbird Motel)

Drag my saddle in and prop it up on the wine-stained carpet. Slight smell of pizza puke coming from the curtains but too tired to care. Crash, sitting on the edge of the mattress. Stare at the perfect acorn oak-leaf pattern carved swirling into the bullhide skirts by gnarly Mexican hands. Always brings some sense of order. Riding the Great Basin for days now, following Jones. Always following Jones. Some grand far-flung plan of his to trap mustangs in canyons. So far all we've seen is their dust. Wiped out. Sore and raw through the knees. Toilet in here keeps moaning and whining like some distant ambulance that will never arrive at the scene of destruction. Forlorn. Flip on CNN just to pretend I'm still in the world. More lies about the war. More exploding roadside goat carcasses. More bodies piling up. I've seen this before. Right next door the casino keeps ringing like churches gone wild. Clanging and churning away. Circus music. What am I hearing? What am I see-

ing from this far edge of the bed? Talons, nicotine-stained finger-
tips digging quarters out of plastic cups. Oxygen running through
green tubes, up the noses of the dead, the already dead. Righteous-
ness ringing its head off. Jackpots of stone. Saddle-soap my tack.
That's it. A job. Give me a job. Glycerine and water. Sip Jack.
Tomorrow we're supposed to meet up with some rancher named
Valmy, west of the Rubies. Unload a Gooseneck jammed with pipe
corral. Panels. Chains and stakes. Rawhide hobbles. Nylon rope.
I'm just not sure about Jones. This whole scheme of his. Whether
he's still got his wits about him. Never was a real market for these
in-bred mongrels. Why mess with them at all when you could start
with a real horse. Quarter horse or at least a grade. Then you've got
all that hauling out to California. Halter-breaking. Round-pen
time. Blindfolds. Scotch hobbles. Sacking them out. Throwing
them down. Canvas tarps. Why go through all the torment? Hospi-
talization. What's the point? Eighty bucks a head? You've got more
diesel in them than that. This room's forty-something right off the
top. What's he thinking? Something romantic maybe. *The Misfits.*
Days gone by? Give me a break. I asked him about it this morning
over black coffee. Just faced him up with it. Asked him what's the
story? Why persist? You know what he comes up with? Some crazy-
ass limerick ditty that he spouts through this raw hangover twinkle
of the eye. Goes like this:

> There once was a cautious old man
> who never romped or played
> he never smoked
> he never drank
> he never had a mate
>
> So when finally he passed away
> his insurance was flat denied
> for since he never had seemed to live
> they claimed he'd never died

Jones cackles till his coughing fit starts up again then hauls his huge frame off the stool and hitches up his Wranglers. His Spanish-rowel spurs and jingle-bobs make their little music as he ambles toward the open door. This time of year the Great Basin air has the smell of high dryness, close to starched shirts. He pauses at the threshold to light a cigarette and blows smoke out across the Humboldt. "Looks like a good morning for it," he proclaims with his back flat to me. "Meet you down at the pens," and he strides off with the Lucky jutting out his jaw. Who am I to refuse?

Llanos

Incredible these pictures of smoke and fire and meat and men sitting around squinting into the gleaming pit drinking heavy stuff
red sticks spitting at their tall tales some true enough some dumb
cracked guitars smells of horse and calves bawling their heads off
for mama behind mesquite pens and one poor fool has actually
brought his cell phone all the way out here and calls his hooker in
Ft. Worth through digital hopeless roaming against the long splash
of stars and yapping dogs in Llanos beyond belief.

Faith, South Dakota

(Interstate 25)

On a hot blue day I'm heading out to Faith where the great saddle horses originate. I'm going to get me one. A buttermilk dun with a quarter-moon brand on his cheek. I've seen him in my dreams. That's right. I've seen him from far away. I'm going to bring him back home and ride him down to get the mail. And when they ask me where he's from, I'll say I bought him out in Faith on a hot blue day.

Reason

I'm not talking to you about horses anymore. You understand absolutely nothing about horses and I'm not talking to you about them.

Then don't.

I won't. I should have known better than to bring them up at all.

I just don't understand why you would need to get another one when you've got a whole pasture full already.

I don't need a reason to need another one.

Apparently not.

Why would I need a reason?

I have no clue.

I just like having them around.

So why don't you get another one then?

I will.

Good.

I don't need a damn reason.

horses racing men
mummies on the mend
what's all this gauze bandaging
unraveled down the stairs
has something come apart
in here
something without end

Man O'War

Man O'War died with an enormous erection that wouldn't go down. It's true. It's well documented. Ask anyone over at the Jot 'Em Down store. After repeated heart attacks at the age of thirty and servicing hundreds of mares, he finally succumbed. But his member remained permanently stiff. His member remembered. Obviously, there were no women present at his modest funeral just on the outskirts of Lexington. A black canvas sheet was draped ceremoniously over the rude appendage. Apparently two or three gentlemen in bowlers found it somewhat offensive, but they couldn't deny his great preponderance.

"Shoe"

William Shoemaker weighed barely a pound when he was born, in an adobe shack south of El Paso. He was hardly breathing as his grandmother gently cradled him in one hand. She put young William in a shoe box then lit the woodstove. She dropped the heavy oven door and placed the shoe box with little Willie in it, there to warm. It was in that shoe box that Willie came back to life and went on to win eight thousand, eight hundred and thirty-three races.

Lightning Man

Met a man in Montana who was struck by lightning right on the top of his head. On the crown. He showed me the scar. It was deep brown, the color of fried beef liver; about the size of a quarter with a little black dot in the center. He had a whole article written up about him in a fish and game magazine and, for weeks, scientists from the university visited his hospital bedside because, I guess, there aren't that many survivors of lightning strikes direct to the head like that. This man was a fishing guide up in the Absaroka mountain range and had taken a group of Japanese tourists out for trout when the sky turned suddenly black and began to crackle with yellow splinters. From long experience in the high country he knew full well to get the hell out of the water in conditions like that and told the tourists to break down their fancy titanium fishing rods and pack them away. As they were trekking out single file across an open field, this guide was in the lead and, being the tallest, the lightning sought him out. A human lightning rod. Later, when they interviewed the foreign fishermen, they all said the guide's whole body lit up with a blue halo as though he were about to be lifted off to heaven. When the lightning escaped the guide's ankle and grounded out, it then traveled down the entire line of Japanese tourists, knocking them all flat, one by one, like bowling pins. They said it happened so fast they didn't know what hit them. There they were, laid out in a line in an open field at the foot of the mountains, thousands of miles from their homeland, next to an American fishing guide with smoke pouring out the top of his head.

These days now, the Lightning Man spends all his time sitting at a workbench in front of a window that looks out on those very same Absaroka mountains. He creates authentic-looking arrowheads with elk-bone tips, turkey feathers, and Osage shafts. He says he's able to stay focused on the work for maybe an hour at a time but that they haven't yet invented a painkiller that can touch the agony that runs like fiery gravity down through his legs.

Somebody told me once the Greeks had invented a magic elixir for chasing away the memory of all suffering and grief.

Saving Fats

"Incredibly violent down there right now," he says to me as he thunks himself into the B seat. I'm sitting in A by the window, minding my own business, perusing the thin *World Traveler* magazine and happen to hover over a glossy Acapulco beach scene; oiled bodies, turquoise water, palm trees—the usual tourist bait. I'm not even contemplating a Mexican trip. "Ten cops killed down there just last week, in fact," he continues. "Kneecaps knocked off. Executed gang-style." He points an index finger to his temple and pulls the trigger with a little click of his tongue.

"Is that right," I say, hoping he'll catch the cold drift, but he rattles right on, oblivious.

"Drugs, cartels—you know. The Big Dogs have moved into the fancy pink villas; taken over the beach, major hotels, the whole damn town. Armed to the teeth too. Easy to get caught in a crossfire. Never even know what hit you." This time I just make a little *hmm* of acknowledgment as he grinds his slab hips from side to side trying to lash the seat belt around his tremendous middle. He's already sweating profusely. I had the feeling he might be a sweater and now, here it comes, oozing from the deep folds in his neck, beading up on his forehead and chin. "Same thing as down in New Orleans," he goes on (although I fail to make the connection). "Looters were armed better than the cops. AK-47s, Glocks, over and under shotguns— Believe me, I was down there."

"Really?"

"Right in the middle of it. Never seen anything like it and I was born and bred down there. Cops just ran away and hid. Not that

131

you could blame them. It became a question of survival—purely. I count myself among the lucky, though. Friend of mine had a boat. Used to be Fats Domino's bodyguard. Had one of those—what do you call 'em?—'torpedo'?—no—'cigarette' boats—you know."

"Cigarette?"

"Yeah—long, skinny orange sucker with some kind of big-ass Buick engine in it, rumbling away—chrome manifolds— Blow you right out of the water you're not careful. Don't know where he copped the fuel. Must've had a tankful already. Anyway, he comes chugging along in this rig and sees me up on the roof of my crib, just clinging like an armadillo, and he honks his horn at me."

"Honks his horn?"

"They have fancy horns, these cigarette boats. Sound like a European sports car. Just blares out with some dumb melody line like from *Goldfinger* or something. As though he's cruising chicks. And here I am, straddled up there on the shingles in my BVDs and don't recognize him from Adam, but he's waving his Hawaiian shirt and yelling for me to jump down into the water and he'll pick me up."

"How high was the water?"

"High! I mean I'm talking up to the dormers and rising and it is some kind of ugly deep blackish-looking shit with all kinds of plastic milk bottles and chunks of car metal and TVs bobbing along—little dogs paddling around in circles with their eyes bugged out."

"So you jumped?"

"Jumped? No, man— Slid! I am not a jumper, as you can plainly see. Slid my sorry ass all the way down into the slimy goo and he come and threw me a line—my friend."

"The bodyguard?"

"That's right."

"Well, that was kind of heroic of him."

"It was, indeed. He's a heroic kinda fella. That's his business. Protection. Security."

"The hero business."

"Exactly. Saved Fats's life too."

"Fats Domino?"

"The very man."

"*The* Fats Domino?"

"Mr. 'Blueberry Hill' hisself."

"Wow, that's hard to believe."

"Why is that hard to believe?"

"Well, I mean, I used to listen to him in high school."

"Didn't we all?"

"I know, but—"

"He lives right down there in Ward Nine. That's where we saved him. Right in his home haunt."

"I heard that he was missing down there—"

"He was but we saved him."

"Same day you—I mean the same day the guy in the orange cigarette boat picked you up?"

"He was headed over there to get Fats already when he saw me clinging to my A-frame."

"So then, once he got you on board, you both sped over to Fats Domino's house and saved him too? Is that what you're saying? Is that what you want me to believe?"

"I don't know about 'sped.' There wasn't much speeding going on because of all the junk in the water. I mean there was full-grown pecan trees and refrigerators blowing by. You wouldn't believe all the crap there was in that water."

"People?"

"What?"

"Many people? Swimming?"

"Bodies. Floating."

"Is that right?"

"You saw the pictures, didn't you? Everybody saw the pictures. Bodies everywhere. Animals. Horses. You just couldn't believe the power of that water."

"I'll bet—"

"You know, the way you normally look at water—just sitting there, flat and blue—pretty, with the sun hitting on it. Or at night, with the moon—kinda peaceful— Makes you want to fall in love or do something stupid? Uh-uh— That water was a raging monster, let me tell you. It was a stone terror."

"And where did you find Fats? Where was he?"

"He was up on his roof too. Same like I was; grabbing on to the chimney bricks and trying to keep his balance. He had some kind of shiny patent leather dress shoes on—you know, the kind with the little black elastic bows. Cute. Musta been on his way to a gig or just come back from one or maybe that's just what he'd been wearing around the house. I don't know. Had the full tux on, though—the whole deal."

"Full tux?"

"Cummerbund, cuff links—the whole nine yards. It was like the whole damn emergency had just caught him completely up short. Didn't want to get any of it wet either. We told him to kick off the shoes so he could get a better grip but he wouldn't. Said he just bought them shoes and they cost more'n the whole suit put together. He started slipping all over that roof on them fancy leather soles—and he's not built for speed, you know—Fats. Built for comfort, just like me—right along the same lines as me. And now the two of us—me and the bodyguard, we're sitting in the boat afraid he's just going to go ass over teakettle off that pitched roof and drown hisself in the gravy. So, finally, we talk him into just setting down on his haunches, nice and easy, and then inching his way to us— Just more less like the way I done it."

"And you got him on board?"

"We did. We managed to hoist him up on that orange cigarette boat, just through pure kindness and coercion. And he was panting kind of heavy and worked up—making funny sounds out his nose. And we could understand that on account of the situation he'd been in and his general kind of—physical condition. You know—being right stout and everything. But then his shoulders start to shake up and down—his huge shoulders, and we see that he's weeping. That's what he's doing—weeping. And we're saying, 'Fats, what's the matter? What's the matter, Fats? You're okay now. You're in the boat. We got you safe and sound now. We're gonna get you outa here.' But he just keeps right on moaning and weeping away like he's lost his mama or something. So I ask him, 'Is there someone left behind in your crib, Fats? Is there anyone else inside there?' And that black water's lapping up around the windows of his little white house and I'm thinking nothing could still be alive inside there because that water's just too damn high and ugly. And then Fats says, 'My piano'—just like that. That's exactly what he says: 'My piano's in there.' And right then—just exactly when he said that, we saw that piano of his go floating on by the front door. It must've busted itself out through a window or something, but there it was—kind of rocking back and forth like a little white city all its own. A baby grand. Just beautiful the way it pitched back and forth like it was playing a little silent waltz to itself. And Fats, when he saw it— I thought he was going to jump right back in the water. We had to hold him down and restrain his ass. He was, by God, ready to jump in and try and save that thing like it was his only child."

"So, did you manage to save it for him? His piano?"

"We got ahold of it. Tied lines to the legs and started towing it real slow, out of the neighborhood, down Caffin Avenue. And you should've seen it—with Fats sitting right back there by the chrome motor, chugging along in his tuxedo and snappy Italian shoes and he never once took his eyes off that baby grand the whole while. Just glued to it like as though he thought if he looked away for a second it might just go down and disappear. And don't you know what happens then— One of the legs of the piano snaps right off. Just as we hit about Montereau Street, trying to make that big loop out past the levee; the leg just cracks itself in half and that piano did a flip and went right under."

"Sank?"

"Completely. And so here we are again— We've got to hold Fats down to the gunwales, he's so excited we're afraid he's gonna capsize the whole bunch of us. He's become one desperate man— crashing around with his eyes just hunting that water for any sign. Then, bam!—here it pops up again, white and shiny with its teeth grinning out at us. We've still got one line on that other leg but it's not tracking with us like it was before. It's causing the whole boat to heave off to one side and the front end is lurching way up like it might just roll over and capsize on top of us. So now, my friend the bodyguard is saying we're going to have to cut the piano loose before we end up drowning the boat altogether and he breaks out one of those SWAT team kind of knives with saw teeth like a shark and Fats is yelling, 'No! No! That's my piano, man! You can't cut my piano loose! I'll never find it again!' And he jumps clean overboard!"

"No!"

"God's truth. Just throws his huge self off the back end of that fancy boat where the motor's churning away and he's thrashing around in his tuxedo trying to dog-paddle over to his sinking piano while my friend shuts the motor off so it won't chop Fats into chunks of meat. And now the boat kind of settles down some and the piano just lurks there in the water with one corner of it sticking up and Fats has found the rope line and is inching his way down it toward the baby grand and talking something—saying something out loud as he's paddling along. I think, at first, he's talking to us but he's not, he's talking to that piano and he's telling it 'Everything is gonna be all right,' in the softest, sweetest voice; 'Everything is gonna be all right, now.' Just talking to it like that. Repeating it like you'd talk to a child stuck high up in a tree and you're trying to climb to it and keep it calm: 'Everything is gonna be all right,' over and over again. And Fat's big head and shoulders are slowly making their way toward the keyboard as he keeps quietly talking to it and the two of us are just holding our breath, waiting to see what happens. What're we gonna do now? We got the engine stopped. We got Fats Domino in the water and we're tied on to a damn baby grand piano, bobbing up and down in that soup while all the guts of New Orleans goes roaring past us toward the Gulf of Mexico."

"So, is the water still rising at that point?"

"Water's leveled off some but it's getting dark and nothing's working. No lights. Electricity's all busted up and fires breaking out everywhere. Power lines snapping and spitting. People screaming. Far away you can hear voices calling out but there ain't nothing you can do. People just come floating by hanging onto their front doors, hunks of blue insulation, Styrofoam, any old piece a junk that floats. You just sit there and watch them come and go. Helpless. You and them, both. Some of 'em you recognize from the neighborhood. You call out to 'em. They call back and drift away. And Fats— Fats, he yells out for us to throw him another line of rope and we're yelling back: 'Fats, you gotta get back in the boat now! We gotta get you outa here! It's getting dark and we gotta find our way out of this mess.' And he says, 'I'm not leaving without my piano, man! I'm not leaving without it!' So we toss him out another line and he catches hold of it and starts wrapping it around his chest and over his cummerbund then tying the end onto another leg of that piano. And we're telling him: 'Fats, don't tie that thing around yourself! If that piano goes down you're gonna for sure drown!' And just right then that's exactly what happens."

"It went under?"

"That piano pulls him right down. They both go under and disappear. And my friend the bodyguard he jumps in after them with his shark-tooth knife and I'm thinking now I'm in really deep shit—alone on the boat and I don't know the first damn thing about how to get it started. I'm hardly familiar with Ward Nine in the dry daylight and now here it is all covered in water and it's getting to be dark thirty. Then, my last thought—and this is the one that freezes my blood up solid. You wanna know what that last thought was?"

"What?"

"Alligators."

"Alligators?"

"Alligators, just lurking. You know they gotta be. There's dead meat everywhere. It's like a cafeteria for alligators. But before I could get too carried away with that, up bobs Fats and the baby grand again, like a dolphin breaking the surface. And Fats is sitting up on the corner of it now, roped to it—just sitting on the bass end of the eighty-eights and he's smiling and spitting water and he laughs with this big old grin: 'Everything is gonna be all right now! Everything is gonna be all right!' And there was just no reason in the world for us to disbelieve him. That piano was riding up on top of the water just as flat as a table and Fats was sitting up there like he was ready for a cocktail and my buddy hauls himself back on board with his knife between his teeth, turns that motor over, and off we go like the tail end of some old beat to shit Mardi Gras."

"And you got him out of there? To safe ground. You saved Fats Domino?"

"And his piano—both."

"That's incredible! You actually saved Fats Domino!"

"That's exactly right— Well—me and my friend did."

"The bodyguard."

"Right."

"That's amazing."

"I can't believe it myself, sometimes."

"You must feel really good about that."

"I do. I actually do."

We're high above Detroit by now, looking down at the sparkling lights just coming on. Then, the dark gray wolf head of Lake Superior begins to emerge out of the northwest. My partner in flight takes a little snack break; tears an edge off a cranberry muffin, pops it in his mouth, then twiddles his fingers to shed the crumbs. He licks the corners of his mouth, preens his moustache and beard, then wipes the moisture from his neck with the linen napkin. His eyes have a gentle, slightly feminine cast with long lashes tucked deep in his chubby cheeks. He tells me this is "Day 52" for him, since the flood. Fifty-two days wandering the country in a Dodge van with nothing but what he had hastily thrown into it as he fled the city of his birth. Since the hurricane he hasn't stopped moving; revisiting ex-wives, girlfriends, relatives, friends of family. From Biloxi to Memphis to Philadelphia to New Jersey, New York; slowly working his way north. Now he's flying out to St. Paul to track down an aunt he last saw when he was ten. He hopes he can still recognize her. She's told him she has an extra bed. Then he might head west, he thinks. He's never been there. Portland or Seattle. "Maybe it's time to get adventurous." I go back to the *World Traveler* just out of having nothing left to say. "I wouldn't recommend Acapulco, though, if I were you," he reiterates, as though *I* were the one in search of new digs. "Dangerous as hell down there."

"No," I say. "I was just thumbing through the pictures."

"Dangerous just about anywhere when you think about it."

"I try not to."

"What's that?"

"Think about it."

"Well, yeah—right. That's probably a good policy. Otherwise you'd just never venture out at all, would you?"

"Probably not." I return the magazine to the pouch on the back of the seat in front of me and reset my chair as we begin our descent into the Twin Cities. My friend nibbles away at his muffin, staring contemplatively straight ahead. He seems gripped by a deep silence now as though his immediate unknown future were a tangible thing; a strange partner he was just now getting used to. Out the window the streaming highway lights frame the braided black headwaters of the Mississippi, laying out placid and lazy in their seedbed before starting the long, inexorable journey south to the Gulf of Mexico. "Can I just ask you one thing?" I say to the man from New Orleans. Again, he twiddles his fingers, knocking crumbs into his lap then flicking them to the floor.

"Sure. Why not?" he says.

"Did all that stuff actually happen? I mean with Fats—saving Fats Domino. Or did you just—kind of dream it all up?" He pauses a moment, staring down at his beefy knees, then looks up at the plastic ceiling as though trying to pierce right through it to the rushing night sky.

"What's the difference?" he says to me.

In Memory of Chappy Hardy
10/05 NYC

Bossier City, Louisiana

(Highway 220)

Ceiling's way too low. Made out of I don't know what. Fireproof sheetrock or something lumpy. Little squares of it squeezed together in sections. Some of the squares don't quite fit. There's black gaps where the wind comes through. I can see it. The wind. I watch it. I'm not sure if it's coming from the outside or inside. Like wind from the building itself. Building-generated wind, I guess. And dust. Tiny floating particles of crud. And bugs. Beautiful long-winged lacy-looking things with bent, delicate legs. They press against the glass sliding door and look like they're licking it. I don't know what could be on the glass that they like to lick it like that. Salt maybe. We're a long way from the sea. Maybe film from the sticky humidity. Maybe something sweet but I can't think what that would be either. There's nothing sweet in here. There's displaced New Orleans people in here, that's for sure. Whole families living all around me. Right next door. Maybe ten people in there. All ages, I guess. You can hear them. Way too many for one squashed-up room. You can hear them trying to get along. Trying to find room to sleep side by side, head to toe, or even a place to sit down with a plate of food. They're cooking all the time in there. You can smell it; crawfish, jambalaya, all that Cajun stuff. They're always cooking seems like. Singing too. But there's fights going on. Somebody pushing somebody else around. Family. Brothers fighting. Sisters-in-law. Mothers yelling. Kids wailing away. Then everyone will suddenly just stop and laugh. Just like that. Amazing how that happens. They'll all just stop and laugh. I never hear the joke, the punch line; just the laughter. Maybe somebody is getting made fun of. I don't know. That could be too. Somebody getting humiliated. That happens. Sometimes you see them coming and going with their laundry or bringing beer into the room—Diet Sprite, stuff like that. You can spot them right away from the people in Shreveport. They stand right out. White bandanas, these exotic print dresses with tropical flowers and parrots flying across their breasts. They sound different too. They've got that different ring that must come from back deep in those bayous somewhere. I don't know. I try not to look them straight in the eyes. I don't know why. I'm not afraid or anything, I just don't want them to think I might be curious about their catastrophe. You know— I don't want to embarrass them. Not that they would be. I wonder about catastrophe sometimes. How close it is. How near. Right here, under the skin. How some people it never seems to touch and other ones that's all they know. Like some of these people here, you see that their whole life has just been a string of catastrophes; one strung on top of another, like bad beads. This hurricane deal is just another one. Maybe the worst but just another one. Who knows, maybe those weren't the first bodies they ever saw floating facedown through the drowning streets. Maybe that wasn't the first time they had to carry their mother on their back or not eat for three days or have to fight off a dog to get something out of a garbage can. Makes you wonder. I lie here sometimes thinking about it. Just lie here watching the overhead fan and listening to all these people. Listening to Highway 220 moaning right outside the sliding glass door. You can see the trucks pouring back and forth from Dallas. You can hear the B-52 bombers big as small cities running low patterns all day long. Running circles from the local air base; practicing for Iraq, I guess. Practicing for some new catastrophe. Something coming up. Maybe they know something we don't. I'm sure they do. We're the last to find out. Don't you think? Always. Big long ropes of black fuel trailing out across the sky, out past Louisiana Downs, across the greasy Red River where the big glitzy casinos flash their neons bragging about jackpots and payouts and fun trips to the Bahamas and nobody out here's got a pot to piss in. Nobody on this side of the river anyway.

Shreveport, Louisiana

train
kind vagrants
strippers
still living with their dazed parents

I haven't turned the TV on in 30 days

next door in 311
a Landman named Stuart left me a note
about how he came to be a cowboy
even though he's not anymore
he's a Landman now
hunting for Natural Gas
he said he hoped he didn't bore me with it
(in the note)

a bottle of fancy Italian wine
with a blue ribbon
sits unopened on the kitchen counter
I have no idea
who even knew I was living here

Casey Moan

I thought I heard that Casey when she moan
I thought I heard that Casey when she moan
She moanin' just like my woman was right on board

John Luther Jones was born in a far-flung corner of southeastern Missouri. At the raw age of thirteen he and his family moved to Cayce, Kentucky, a town I can't even locate on my Rand McNally road map. Evidently, it was directly across the rolling junction of the Ohio and Mississippi rivers from Cairo, Illinois, the most important port town for the transportation of Union troops during the Civil War; one of only four gateways between the northern railways and the Deep Southern slave states. Its strategic location, according to one account, made Cairo "like a loaded pistol aimed down the Mississippi at the throat of the lower Confederacy." More than twenty years after the end of the war, the young Jones sat entranced on the banks of the wide river watching the comings and goings of the Illinois Central locomotives as they loaded and unloaded the flat white ferryboats heading down to New Orleans. Their long feathery plumes of steam seemed to hang forever above the dark water, beckoning him toward an irresistible destiny. Soon, he became a fireman on the Illinois Central, stoking the raging stoves of the engines as they carried huge crowds up to Chicago for the World's Columbian Exposition at Jackson Park. Before long the kid had picked up the moniker "Casey" from his hometown in Kentucky and his frame had grown as tough as the cordwood he fed the voracious boilers. In February of 1890, while not quite twenty-six years of age, Casey Jones was promoted to engineer and became famed for being able to play a fancy tune on the locomotive's six-tone calliope whistle. His favorite was the Stephen Foster classic, "My Old Kentucky Home." Early in January of 1900, Casey was again promoted to the Memphis–Canton run, aboard the fastest passenger train ever built: *The Cannonball Express*. Shortly before midnight on April 29, 1900, Jones and his trusty fireman, Sim Webb, were asked to take the southbound *Cannonball* out of Memphis, even though they had just finished a regular northbound run into the city, and were dog tired. When Casey pulled out of the Memphis station for the 188-mile run back south to Canton, Mississippi, the six-car passenger train was already ninety-five minutes late. Jones was not a man to be tardy and he urged Sim Webb to feed the dragon in earnest. As they rocketed through the night, down through the deep hardwood forests of Mississippi, the *Cannonball* soon devoured the lost time. Just outside Vaughan, a tiny outpost fourteen miles north of Canton, a strange combination of fates was awaiting them: the wide-open throttle of Casey's engine, a broken air hose on a freight train stalled on the track up ahead, and the total absence of block signals on the southern line. As Casey went to the brake, he yelled at Sim Webb to jump clear. The screaming flanged steel wheels showered sparks through the dark woods. Casey stuck to his post. Sim Webb jumped to safety. No other crew member or passenger sustained more than a minor injury. But Casey was gone.

Mr. Williams

I'm telling you, he was dead standing up. Stone dead. I was there. Room #17, Andrew Johnson Hotel, Knoxville, 1953. I was right there with him in the room. Me, propping him up on one side and that driver-guy, that chauffeur of his, on the other. Believe his name was Carr, that driver. Charlie Carr. I remember all that. Don't ask me how. Can't even remember what I had for breakfast but I can remember all that back then clear as a brass bell. Sticks in your mind. A thing like that—dressing up a dead man in a fresh suit of clothes. I'm telling you, like a rag doll he was. And, all the time we're putting the clothes on him that driver-guy, that Carr fella, thinks he's still alive. Even called a doctor up to the room to give him a shot of morphine and B_{12}. On top of all the beer and whiskey he had in him already—pills and whatnot. Man was a mess. I think it was that doctor killed him, tell you the damn truth. That's what I think because he was sure as shine dead when we was putting that fresh suit of clothes on him. Dead as a post. Made a noise, though. Kind of a rasping sound came out of him like wind rustling dry leaves. That's probably why Carr thought he still had some life left in him. But all that is is the death rattle. That's all that is. Air escaping the corpse, like some ghost getting the hell out the door before it slams shut. I've heard that sound before, believe you me. You see lots of comings and goings being a porter in a hotel like that. You see it all. Whores knifed in the face. Suicides. Had two young kids jump right out of a window once, on the eighth floor.

Jumped right out the damn window, holding hands. Boy and girl. Must've been nineteen, twenty years old is all. Girl was pregnant too. That's the shame of it. But Mr. Williams—laying there like a stick. Never forget that. Got him all decked out in that new suit; bright blue with a fresh white shirt, yellow tie—little green palm tree embroidered right in the middle of it. All this stuff gets imprinted on your mind, for some reason. Shiny black boots made in Ft. Worth with musical notes and little gold guitars stitched into the leather, dancing all across the toe and heel. His cream white Stetson we set crown down on the bed beside him after we flopped him over on the mattress. That's when that sound came out of him. He was flat dead, though, so help me, God. You could tell by the way he landed. But that driver-guy, that Charlie Carr, keeps saying he's got to get him back in the Cadillac downstairs. He's got some gig to make in Canton, Ohio, somewheres—some roadhouse or theatre or other. I don't know. Had about two hours to make the show, he said. So we haul him up off the bed and prop him up again; throw his dead arms around our shoulders, squash that Stetson down on his head, and off we go, out the door, down the stairs, boots dragging and banging down every step till we get to the lobby. Desk clerk cracks wise as we go past about how Mr. Williams may have had one too many. We laughed about it, me and Carr, trying to make it all slide by; go along with the game. But I regret that now—that laugh. Man was dead after all. Dead in his boots. We got him out on the street through the revolving door and I remember how the streetlamp lit up that bright blue suit of his. Blue must've been his favorite color because that Caddie was blue too. Kind of a light powder blue like a robin's egg. Carr opened the back door with his free hand and we slid Mr. Williams in, gentle as we could and here comes that awful sound out of him, one last time. I remember thinking then, that's a terrible sound to come out of a man, like that. Man who spent his whole short lifetime singing like a beautiful bird. That's a terrible, terrible sound.

Five Spot

I studied Eric Dolphy nightly, very close up, front row sometimes. 1963–64; something like that. Watched his listening; ramrod straight spine on a tall oak stool, like a monk, like a regal jaybird; black bass clarinet (or was it soprano sax?) hung between his knees, hung from a loop around his neck; eyes pinned to the bandstand floor, seeing right through it while Mingus mashed away with his meaty fingers, cruel smile. Jaki Byard, Dannie Richmond; "Fables of Faubus." Dolphy's Egyptian pharaoh goatee, long with a knob at the end, hieroglyphic, staring into the next phrase; seeing it coming up, seeing right into his death, in a matter of days. The dismay on Mingus's face on return without him. Leaving Dolphy's body behind in Germany, on tour; failed blood, medical inattention. The disbelief, the vacancy, the awful hole where he used to lift his licorice horn to the heavens and sail away, past the old Five Spot café, which is now a dumb-ass Pizza Hut.

Knoxville, Tennessee

(Highway 40)

How do you "teach" yourself anything? Assuming one part of you knows something that another part of you may not; some magical suspicion. In matters of the voice (aside from purely physical limitations like the size of the windpipes or the shape of the mouth and nasal cavities), is there possibly some territory of the imagination which might "inform" the singing of a song; shaping it to fit the timbre and character of a more legendary voice, such as Dr. Ralph Stanley possesses. Not an imitation of Ralph Stanley but a kind of incantation. I've been driving down through the mountains of Tennessee, below the Cumberland Gap, ripping my throat out trying to sing just like Dr. Stanley; repeating the track of an ancient recording he must have made on the back porch of his cabin in Virginia. In the background you can hear screen doors slapping, a baby cry, a distant dog, and intermittent blasts of cicadas. The song itself is far more ancient than the recording; an a cappella hymn called "Poor Pilgrim" that must have come across the great ocean with the first wave of Scotch-Irish immigrants. These are the haunted lyrics:

I soon shall reach the bright glory
where mortals no more complain

The old ship is approaching
the Captain is calling my name

Sometimes I'm tossed and I'm driven
and know not where to roam

But I've heard of a city called heaven
and I've started to make it my home

Hark, what is that I see coming
my blood's running cold and slow

But Jesus can quiet the Jordan
and pilot me through as I go

It's impossible to depict on paper the extraordinary leaps of modulation and uncanny phrasing that Stanley's voice carves through every word and line; tailing each verse with a light "yip" harking back to certain old sea chanties like "Blood Red Roses" which the early sailors sang with foreboding rounding Cape Horn through terrible currents, on their way to the Gold Rush. This same "yip" later found its way unfathomably into the campfires of cowboys in Texas, singing to the moon and stars, and must have even influenced the high yodeling of Jimmie Rodgers and Hank Williams, much later. Everything has its heritage. Sad to say, but the modal style of singing that Ralph Stanley embodies (which is not a style at all but a belief; a way of life) has all but died in this era of "sampling" and electronic voicings. The only other place I've heard anything like it was in a pub called The Cobblestone in Ireland where a man named Seamus Fitzpatrick stood up in the middle of the day and began a twenty-seven-verse ballad in the Sean-nóis tradition in honor of his dead father. The entire pub went silent with bowed heads toward the black pints of Guinness except for those who knew the song from childhood and seamlessly joined Seamus, not missing a word of the tale. By the end of the twenty-seventh verse, the sun was just beginning to set through the tobacco-stained windows, and the melody still hung heavy in the air.

Head in the World

I had ideas for sure, the night before, of what it might be like. Projections. Pictures, I guess. In my head. Of what my head would be like. Severed like that. Suddenly cut off. Separate. Certainly, no one else can tell you what it's like. Run the gauntlet and come back to tell the tale. Except me. Perhaps. Too soon to tell. I could be the only one. Who knows? You'd have to comb the planet looking for evidence. Could it be? I'm the only one. Certainly not. I don't know. It's beyond me somewhat. Now. I mean, now. Being out in the world. Out and about. Being out in the thick of things with no body at all. Just rolling around. No precedent. But nevertheless, things ran through my mind the night before the execution. If you want to call it that. My mind inside my head. Things running wild in there. Make no mistake. You can just imagine. The gleaming blade. The white neck. Anticipation. How do you describe it? The clean break. I had heard rumors that the suddenness of it, the abrupt clash of steel on bone caused a continuation, a certain suspension of belief that the two might still be connected. The head and body. The link of the neck. Like the way both halves of a rattler will keep twisting once you've cut him in two. Chicken running around with his head cut off. That kind of thing. Or the way they say Mary Queen of Scots's head kept chattering for a full fifteen minutes afterward as the executioner marched up and down the scaffold presenting it to the crowd, clutching it by its thick red curly hair; eyes wide open, jaw and lips snapping up and down with no words. As though the head still belonged to the living; some last expression of self, a desperate attempt at being. I don't know. I wasn't there. These things are hard to describe when you get right down to it. "Suspended"? "Floating"? Nothing quite nails it down. It was immediate, though. I'll say that much. Not unlike the hackneyed magician's trick where he jerks the entire tablecloth out from under the plates and saucers and they all remain exactly where they are. Something like that. Or the way all the lights in the city go black and suddenly everyone's silent. Everyone waiting for the world to fall away but it already has.

It's curious, though—this vague yearning for home. This yearning for place. Some place or other. Why would that be? When it's all said and done. Why a lake, for instance, when I came from the desert? Heat and sand. Why a lake for Christ's sake?

Suddenly

Suddenly—the word most used by Dostoyevsky. Somebody told me that. Some Dostoyevsky expert. *Suddenly.* As though any kind of action could be drawn into words: Suddenly music. Suddenly turning. Suddenly silent. Suddenly. As though I never saw the process.

Everyone in the old house is sick but me. Silence, except for the snoring, coughing, and occasional trips to the bathroom. Snow everywhere through the windows. You can't look out without seeing it. Suddenly winter. Frozen rivers. Bitter cold. Barren trees. Small silver plane etched out against a chalk, still sky. Suddenly, completely alone.

Tall Thin White Man

A tall thin white man in wire-rimmed glasses (from the thirties) stands in front of a mirror shaving his ears with an electric razor; mouthing words to himself (or someone else, we're not sure), mouthing something to someone who is not there, unseen, imaginary (most likely a woman although this information is more for the actor than anyone else).

·   ·   ·   ·   ·

A naked, skinny, tall white man, well past middle age, stands in front of a mirror which is hanging from an invisible wire (possibly very light monofilament fishing leader) shaving his ear and nose hair; trimming his short sideburns then, squeezing some white cream out of a tube, he rubs it gently on his nose and starts speaking to an imaginary woman but in mime. The only sound is the sound of the electric razor.

·   ·   ·   ·   ·

A tall thin white man in glasses, well past middle age with a pot-belly, white boxer shorts with his balls hanging out one side very visibly; white sleeveless T-shirt identical to the one worn by Paul Newman in *Hud* (or was it *The Hustler*?). In any case, the tightness of the sleeveless T-shirt only accentuates the pot of his belly. He is meticulously shaving his ears, nose hair, shortish sideburns and spends a great deal of time on one pesky black curled-up hair protruding from the top of his cheekbone (which the audience can't see).

. . . . .

Periodically (not often) the tall thin white man shuts the razor off and speaks out loud to an imaginary woman, imploring her to reconsider her quick departure. He goes so far as to admit he misses her deeply even though she's just recently walked out the door and clicked it quietly shut, intentionally avoiding the provocative slam. (This could all be improvised providing the actor doesn't get too cute with it; pretending he's a writer.)

. . . . .

An extremely tall (well over 6 feet 7 inches) thin, aging white man with a potbelly, sleeveless T-shirt, white boxer shorts, balls hanging nearly to his knees, stands in blank space (no set of any kind), side-lit with no music, staring blankly at the audience (no emotion can be read on his face), arms hanging limply at his side, one hand holding an electric razor, which is turned on, making a sound more like a dentist's drill or a distant chain saw, maybe. After a while (not too long) he turns the razor off and there's silence except for the sporadic coughing and nervous twitching of the audience, which gradually shifts to fascination as the tall thin white man's stare becomes more and more specific and it begins to be clear that he is examining his own face in an imaginary mirror, picking at dry red spots on his nose that seem to have suffered from extreme exposure to the sun or wind or both or just abject neglect. He pulls a tube of cream out of his white boxer shorts, squeezes some out on his finger then rubs it on his scaly nose, then rubs some on his hanging balls. His nose turns white as a lightbulb. His balls turn blue. Now he begins talking out loud to an imaginary woman who seems to have recently departed. He explains in detail the great gaping hole she has left in his chest (which the audience can't see) and how impossible it will be to continue without her. His blue balls start blinking. Then his white nose. They blink in alternating syncopation.

He turns the electric razor back on and shaves his ears, his nose hair, and his short sideburns. In the course of this methodical procedure the lights (pale blue) fade very slowly to black. No music of any kind. The razor continues in the dark. The tall thin white man's balls and nose keep blinking in the pitch black. They blink incessantly until the audience has entirely cleared out.

Perpetual Warrior

That's what he called himself, if you could believe it—The Perpetual Warrior. Bragged about it in all the bars. Said, now that there was perpetual warfare he ought to fit right in. Then he'd laugh and spit into the sawdust floor; fire back another shot of Jameson. He'd elaborate on something he called "a carefully developed spell" against sudden pain. That's how he described it to all the women. The kind of pain that comes unannounced and shocks the entire body, mind, and spirit. Unimaginable pain. Then he'd go on in detail about how the power of this spell was contained inside the rhymes and rhythms of an ancient Icelandic poem called *Song of the Spear,* handed down for centuries from the Battle of Clontarf. According to legend, on the morning before the conflict, twelve Valkyries sat astride their war ponies chanting the poem in unison. The wind off the Irish Sea blew their braided bloodstained hair. The severed heads impaled on the tips of their lances spun in a ragged counterclockwise harmony. The sound was like the humming of a distant hurricane. Huge ravens floated in and out between the shoulders and shields of the warrior women. When they had finished their incantation they rode off through the air toward the battlefield to ordain the ones to be slain.

He would go on like this for hours, in a whiskey reverie, somehow always managing to seduce some stray wild-eyed girl, vulnerable to epic exaggeration.

Livingston, Montana

"Now, try not to be abrupt with her," she says to me on the phone, already coaching and getting me on the defense. "She's a very nice woman and she's just trying to help us out."

"Help us what?" I say. "Where the hell are you, anyway?"

"I told you, we're at the airport and this woman—Mrs. Adams is her name—she just wants to verify with you that Jackson is our son and that you're allowing him to travel with me to Mexico."

"Who is she?"

"She's one of the customs officials here. She just wants to know whether you've given permission for him to go out of the country."

"How does she know for sure that I'm his father?"

"You're going to tell her."

"But I could be anyone."

"But you're not. You're his father."

"But you could have called up anyone and told her that I was the father when I might not be."

"Try, for once, not to be so difficult and just cooperate with me, would you? Just this once."

"I am cooperating."

"All right, now I'm going to put her on. Her name is Mrs. Adams."

"Mrs. Adams. Right. Put her on."

"Try to be nice."

"Just put her on."

"Here she is." A very flat, public-servant voice announces herself through my tequila haze as I swing both legs out of bed and stare at the blank wall of the Masonic Temple across the street.

"Good morning, Mr. Noland, my name is Becky Adams and I'm the Notary Public here at Newark Airport and we need to have your approval that Jackson Noland is your lawful son and that you've given full permission for him to travel out of the country to Mexico with his mother, Jasmine Macey."

"Who?" I say, fumbling for my lighter by the digital clock.

"Jasmine Macey," she repeats.

"Never heard of her."

"You've never heard of Jasmine Macey?"

"That's right. Sounds like a fake name to me. A made-up name, doesn't it?"

"She claims to be the mother of your son, Jackson Noland, and she intends to take him with her to Mexico."

"Well she's lying and I'm not giving any kind of damn permission. Put her back on—this woman, whoever she is. I want to speak to her."

"What's going on?" the mother of my son says. "What did you tell her?"

"Why are you going to Mexico?" I ask her.

"What do you mean, why am I going to Mexico? It's Christmas. We've already been through this. I told you months ago I was going to Mexico for Christmas."

"No you never did."

"What did you tell Mrs. Adams?"

"I told her I never heard of you."

"Oh, great. That's just great! You son of a bitch! What is the matter with you? What kind of a fucked-up mess are you, anyway?"

"I'm pretty fucked up."

"It's your son! This is about your son!"

"You don't need to go to Mexico for Christmas."

"We've had this planned! I bought the tickets, you asshole!"

"Why don't you come out here instead? You'd like it out here. Jackson would—"

"I'm not going out to the wilds of Montana in the middle of winter! Are you nuts?"

"Why not? It's nice. The air is crisp."

"It's freezing out there!"

"Just come out and give it a whirl."

"So, you're refusing to give permission? Is that the story?"

"I don't know why you have to be going to Mexico for Christmas."

"You know what?" she says. "I hate you. I hate everything about you. I always have."

"That figures," I say, as she slams the phone in my ear. The sun brightens the plaster wall of the Masonic Temple. I'm thinking about getting to my feet. I'm thinking about telling my legs to straighten up and climb into my jeans. Sending the signal from my soggy brain to my swelly feet. I'm fishing for my cigarettes. Her voice goes off in my head like a PA system from a squad car: "YOU KNOW WHAT? I HATE YOU! I HATE EVERYTHING ABOUT YOU! I ALWAYS HAVE!"

Lost Whistle

Last night when we were sleeping
I dreamed I lost your big black dog
I searched for him through a town I didn't recognize
People on the street were selling old cracked furniture
looking broke

I tried whistling for your black dog
I tried over and over again to whistle
but something had gone wrong between my teeth and lips
the breath wouldn't channel
nothing came out but a hiss

I hunted desperately with a rising panic
maybe more for the loss of my whistle than your dog
my whistle that had long been with me since I was a kid
I blew and blew
but there was no way your dog could have ever heard it

I came to the top of a hill
out of breath
a white stucco house with an open corridor
a woman sitting there folding laundry
in neat piles

When she saw me she stood and cried out:
Charles! Charles!

Day out of Days

but then realized I wasn't Charles
and began apologizing wildly
wiping her hands on her apron

I told her I was searching for a big black dog
but she didn't seem the least bit interested
as though she'd never heard me
just rambled on about how she talks to herself all the time now
how she can't stop talking to herself

She followed me back down the hill
babbling the whole while
I couldn't get rid of her

Then you woke up and nudged me right in the ribs
asked me why was I tossing and turning
I tried falling back asleep with no success
all I could think about was my lost whistle

A hole opened up in my chest

She

Him? No. Are you kidding? He'll wind up just like his father. You wait and see. Babbling away to himself in the corner of some motel lobby in Lubbock. They'll wonder where he came from. How he arrived. What he was doing in the middle of the day with no ID, no phone, no recollection whatsoever of who he was or where he was headed. They'll give him a bowl of soup and a job washing windows with a squeegee but he won't even last a day. You wait and see. He'll wind up just exactly like his old man. Dead on the side of the road with no witness. I can see it clear as day.

Majesty

(Highway 101 South)

We stop in a place called Smith's in Paso Robles and order turkey gumbo soup and lemon meringue pie with black coffee. This ensemble somehow fits together although it sounds as though the tastes might clash. The theme from *Godfather I* is playing on the jukebox; very dreary and always reminds me of that shocking scene with the decapitated horse head. What goes on in Coppola's mind? How could a guy come up with that? You must have to be Sicilian or something. The skinny waitress here has the worst skin I've seen in a long, long time. She seems to be drowning in Clearasil, poor thing. Already suffering and she's barely sixteen. The decor in here is very weird: old-time meat hooks hanging from the ceiling, unless maybe they're ice hooks. Either way it's incongruous for a roadside café, it seems to me. After blowing laboriously on his gumbo soup, Dennis, out of the blue, starts telling me how his aunt had a stroke recently and can't remember the names of things. Some sort of aphasia or something. She seems to recognize the object itself but can't remember the correct name for it. Like *door* might become *key* in her mind or *dog* might turn into *bug*. Close but way off. I remember that happened to me once when I was a kid—not a stroke but the confusion about naming a thing. My mother became very alarmed about it and marched me over to the icebox. She threw the door open and began hauling out things like a cube of margarine, for instance, holding it up close to my face and demanding that I pronounce the name of it. I knew it wasn't butter because we never had butter but I couldn't remember the other name so I called it "majesty." I remember the panic on her face; as though she suddenly thought she had a cabbage-head for a son on top of everything else she was worried about like the old man and taxes and the price of milk. I think it may have also been the extreme heat back then. We were having one of those desert heat waves that summer where it would sit and swelter around a hundred and twelve at midnight for days on end. No rain. And this was in the time before air-conditioning was even thought of. The hills were all black and smoky from wildfires and when you breathed in you could taste the ash on the back of your tongue. At night I would have dreams where the clouds would just ignite into flames. Anyway, I don't know why it was I suddenly had this little spell of not knowing what to call things. It didn't last long but it was as strange to me as it must have been for my mother. I absolutely could not remember the name for margarine. That's all there was to it.

Bright Spots

Yet another frantic futile car alarm. Shrieking sequence. Vacuumed up the street. A long hollow moan like you're listening just after your heart stops cold. Somewhere above the body, looking down. Maybe on the ceiling. Sometimes I picture bright spots on roads way west. Clearings. Round bales and barns caved in from nothing more than time. That's all. Nothing more than wind and rain. No telling why these fleeting spots come surging up. Could be just the eyes aging. Spots and wriggles. Little white worms projected on the retina. Or maybe it's the mind hunting for another way out. Just seeking the blacktop once again. Flight, is all.

High Noon Moon

(Highway 152, *continued*)

It got pitch black on the highway and the moon was cut in two.
Dennis said it had to be right in between full and new; a kind of
High Noon moon. Dennis has studied these things. We turned off
101 at El Capitán Beach, went under a viaduct, but couldn't find the
ranch sign we were looking for. We stopped by a Little League
baseball diamond and took a leak. (It must have been for Little
League because the fences seemed short.) We pissed in silence. The
moon was the only light around. We could hear the surf crashing
out past the wooden bleachers but couldn't see the white breakers
in the dark. I could picture them though and that seemed enough.
The wind smelled like seaweed and dead fish. We piled back in the
Chevy and finally found Doug's ranch two miles farther down the
road. Doug was one of those guys I'd known from high school
who'd wanted to train Thoroughbreds but wound up running a
beat-up boarding stable out here on the edge of nowhere. We went
into his kitchen and asked Doug's wife who had won the 49er-
Giants game since we hadn't seen a TV in days. She was fixing salad
at the sink and told us she was not a fan of baseball. We tried to
explain it wasn't baseball but then quickly gave up on her. You
could tell she already had her mind set against us and the bad
influence we were about to bring on her husband. Then John and
Dennis got involved in a card game with Doug around a heavy iron
table with blue and yellow Moroccan tile on top and a bottle of
light amber bourbon set next to a candle. I think it might have

been Woodford Reserve. I'm sure it wasn't whiskey though because Doug made a big distinction between the two. He was quite the connoisseur about bourbon, saying it was in an entirely different class because of the Kentucky springwater it was made from. Same water that made the strong-boned racehorses that won the Kentucky Derby; fed from deep limestone aquifers that pulled calcium and mineral nutrients up through the bluegrass where the horses grazed and switched their long black tails. I remember as a kid wondering why in the racing program, every horse that seemed to win a major stake at Santa Anita was bred and raised in Kentucky. I'd never been east of the Mississippi, back then.

I had no interest in blackjack so I walked down to the stable under the cut moon and visited Doug's horses. A barn owl looked straight down at me from the rafters with his big white bib. A Tibetan monk once told me that the owl was a portent of death but I've never felt that way about owls. As I stared at the bright yellow eyes I realized it was a dummy, planted to scare away mice and varmints. It fooled me, that's for sure.

Next day, in L.A. we check into the Tropicana and call home. "Home." I'd forgotten about home. Reporting in to the women on our whereabouts. I'm not sure how curious they've been, to tell the truth. Quite possibly they were glad to get rid of us for a while. Here we are, the three of us in a room the size of a shoe box, taking turns on the phone; staring out through the sliding glass doors at the steaming swimming pool and the palm trees. My wife tells me that Marin and Sonoma counties have completely flooded. Three straight days of torrential rains. They're calling it a disaster zone in the news. Hard to believe since we hadn't experienced even a drizzle the whole way down. All the women and children are totally stranded on the second floor of the house with all the dogs. The basement is under three feet of water. After we hang up, John remembers his collection of rare pornography, his Time-Life historical photography books, and, of course, his precious Ansel Adams sitting on pine board shelves below the water level. He calls back and asks my wife to move them to a higher shelf since his wife would refuse to go anywhere near them. She tells him she's going to have to put on rubber boots and a bikini to get this done and what if the books were already completely ruined? She'd be wasting her time. John tells her he thinks they'll eventually dry out if she'd just please make the effort. He even offers to pay her. After he hangs up I suddenly remember the flood we'd had up there two or three years ago where one of the neighbors had been instantly electrocuted when she swung out of bed and hit the water with bare feet. An electric fan plugged into the wall was sending out a deadly current. I call back and tell my wife to make sure she checks the water first before stepping into it. She asks me how she's supposed to do that without getting a shock and I suggest she throw one of the dogs in and see what happens. Very funny, she says, and hangs up on me just like the Mexican women up in San Juan. Now Dennis calls home but there's no answer. He lets it ring for a long, long time. Now I remember that my family album from my dad's side of the family is also in the basement, probably well below flood level. Why would I suddenly feel this strange attachment toward these ancient crumbling brown photos of my great-grandmother sitting on a buckboard wagon behind two dark plow horses, struggling through deep mud somewhere in rural Illinois; my father as a little boy, no shirt, smiling brightly with a string of perch; my mother feeding pigeons from an army Jeep? But then I pull myself together and drop all these pictures in my head and see exactly what's right in front of me: our white feet on the green synthetic carpet, our empty hands, and our fatherless faces.

Orange Grove in My Past

I thought I had done my level best, done everything I possibly could, *not* to become my father. Gone out of my way in every department: changed my name, first and last, falsified my birth certificate, deliberately walked and swung my arms in exact counterpoint to the way he had; picked out clothing the opposite of what he would have worn, right down to the underwear; spoke without any trace of a Midwestern twang, never kicked a dog in the ribs, never lost my temper over inanimate objects, never again listened to Bing Crosby after Christmas of 1959, and never ever hit a woman in the face. I thought I had come a long way in reshaping my total persona. I had absolutely no idea who I was but I knew for sure I wasn't him.

Then, in the fall of '75, I discovered a bottle of Hornitos tequila; pure white, green label. I just stumbled across it like you do some women. I was swept off my feet. I became so completely enraptured that the rest of the world fell away and I never heard the pounding on my door until it was too late. As I reached for the knob to see who it was the entire door exploded and came off its hinges. My father crashed in through the splinters, face red, enraged, and threw me up against the wall. He demanded to know why I had forsaken him. Why I had trained myself to walk the way I did, speak the way I spoke, wear the kind of clothes I wore and why in the world I had never gotten married. My mouth was dry. I told him in a whisper that I had no answers to any of it. I had no reasons. I was as dumbfounded as he was. The red washed out of his face. He stood there and stared at me for a long time then a slight smile appeared but it wasn't for me. It was an "I'll be darned" kind of a smile and I half expected him to scratch his head but he didn't. He just turned and stood there with his back full to me and looked through the ripped-out door frame to the orange orchard across the road in perfect weedless rows. The sweet smell of the blossoms made me feel like throwing up. The perfume was every-where that time of year. He walked away from me, straight toward the orange trees, and kept the same steady pace as he crossed the road. A car almost hit him but he never wavered. The driver leaned on the horn and kept it up all the way down to the highway. You could hear the horn fading away as my father disappeared between the trees.

Kingman, Arizona

(Andy Devine Boulevard)

I distinctly remember Andy Devine on a little bay horse in the Rose Parade, back in 1950-something. He played a character called Jingles on black-and-white TV. A big convivial man, always grinning and waving. He'd cock his wrist on top of his immense belly and twiddle his fingers as though he were tickling you from a distance. The gesture was reminiscent of Oliver Hardy. In fact Andy could well have "borrowed" it from Oliver. They both had the same impish smile too. Andy was the proverbial sidekick and always rode between Roy Rogers and Dale Evans, who were very straight and proper; their fringed Western outfits pressed and glittering with rhinestones. They rode ramrod straight in their matching silver concho saddles while Andy slouched in his plain old bullhide one. I don't know if the slouch was put on or if it was an actual manifestation of his character but he seemed to enjoy being a sloppy guy. He liked his juxtaposition. He had a high squeaky voice that my uncle Buzz told me was the result of Andy's having accidentally swallowed a silver whistle when he was a kid. I always believed that story. Why not?

Van Horn, Texas

(Highway 10)

Little waitress doesn't get it when I push my half-eaten steak away and ask her for dessert, that I really want dessert. She thinks there's something wrong with the steak. There's nothing wrong with the steak. I'm just ready for dessert. Another thing she doesn't get is that I have enough cash in my left boot right now to buy a small car or half the town and when I ask her if she wants to take a spin around the dusty block she doesn't understand that either. She thinks I have ulterior motives. I tell her I've just come from the "Land of Milk and Honey." She backs nervously away with my half-eaten steak on the plate and bumps right into the chef coming out of the swinging chrome doors of the kitchen. Chef wants to know what's wrong with my steak and I tell him nothing—nothing's wrong with the steak. All I want is dessert and she giggles as though the implication is that she's the "dessert" and the chef picks up on this and decides I'm seriously demented road trash and starts asking me to leave. I tell him I haven't finished my lunch yet and that I was very much looking forward to the butterscotch pie. He says the pies just came out of the oven and they're too hot to cut and I tell him I don't mind waiting but he says he can't cut into any of them because it would sacrifice the whole pie just trying to get a single slice out of it. I tell him, sometimes sacrifice is necessary. I can see them all steaming behind him on a Formica shelf; lined up like little locomotives—puffing away. He tells me it's going to take quite a while. It's going to be at least an hour. I tell him that's fine, I'll just go out and buy a paper and come back. I'll stroll around the town and take in the sights. He says there are no sights; there is no town. But I tell him I'm a big fan of desolation. I'm fascinated by the way things disintegrate; appear and disappear. The way something very prosperous and promising turns out to be disappointing and sad. The way people hang on in the middle of such obliteration and don't think twice about it. The way people just keep living their lives because they don't know what else to do. He says he has no time for small talk and leaves me staring at the sugar.

Mercenary Takes a Stab at Self-Improvement

One day he thought he'd try to control his nagging tendencies toward anger and arrogance, cruelty and malice, by reminding himself that he wouldn't live forever and that everything he saw squirming in front of him would soon vanish from the earth. When that didn't work he tried allowing the sweet sensations of nature to penetrate his tough hide: glittering morning sunlight speckled through the drifting ginkgo leaves, for instance; the cool breeze playing across his ragged face; distant sounds of children rollicking in the schoolyard. When that didn't work he began conjuring up memories of sexual conquests, going clear back through his teenage years; girls came floating back to him; girls of all sizes, tinged now and then with the glowing aura of love. Whatever that was. What was that? Had he mistaken something temporarily ecstatic for something else? Something lasting? Or was he just getting all worked up in a lather of delusion? How easy it was to get carried away. Erection and all. When that seemed to lead nowhere he tried the old trick of total acceptance. Relinquishing completely to the two-sidedness of his nature. He bucked and whined through it. The warp and weave, as they say; trying to catch his balance, crashing then retrieving the old goose step as good as new. When that wore out he tried the impossible mental exercise of putting himself in the place of another; walking in their proverbial shoes; seeing the inevitable end of civilization through their eyes. The horror show with a twist, if you like. When all that finally failed he chopped off his left index finger just below the first knuckle after the manner of the Arapaho ritual of grief over ancestors lost in battle. He wrapped the gushing wound in oak leaves and held it high above his head, squeezing it tight with his right hand. His good hand. The hand he wrote with. He tried to restrain his breath from galloping away.

Interview in Café Pascual

So—sounds, say—favorite sounds.

Um—mockingbird. Meadowlark. Crickets, for sure. Distant hounds.

Hounds?

Yes.

Like dogs, you mean?

No, hounds.

In people's yards or what?

No, hunting. Chasing.

Game?

That's it. Wild things. Pigs mostly.

I see. And that reminds you of days gone by, does it?

Yes.

When was that? When were these days?

Day out of Days

When I was a hunter.

Did you kill things back then?

Yes. I ate them.

Meat.

Yes.

How long ago was this?

Long, long ago.

In the distant past?

Memory fails me.

But you have faint tracings?

Hardly anything comes back.

So, you gave it up?

It just left me.

So what did you replace it with?

What.

Hunting—following the hounds.

Nothing.

But what do you do with yourself now?

I wander around from place to place.

Aimlessly?

What's there to aim for?

That must get old after a while.

I don't know what else to do.

June Bugs

Someone hunting in the night. Shooting repeatedly along my tree-line. Dull sudden thuds, then blank. Then shots again. Someone wanting something dead. Each time the shots come I see his finger squeezing down: fat, black and blue, oily knuckle. In the pauses nothing moves but the fan and night bugs. Out of nowhere, hard little red June bugs come crashing into the porch light, hit the screen door, and go crashing to the floor. They're all around me now, spinning on their backs, dying between my bare cracked feet. I'm just sitting here and this happens. It's beyond belief.

Herdbound

Horses are calling each other across big acres. Acres of fresh-cut hay where the tractor's stripes lay dark and flat against the blue-grass morning. These are the fastest horses in the world. These are the horses the Arabs want, the Irish, the English, the Germans. The whole world converges on this tiny spit of Dixie limestone to throw money in the air as if it were confetti. These horses don't know their day is coming to wear a paste-on hip number and parade in tight circles while the bid-spotters scream and their sale electronically climbs into the millions. Those anonymous bidders don't see them now, the way they are, racing along black fence lines, screaming across stands of hickory and locust; sensing something in the air, something coming to get them, from far far across the high seas.

Nine Below

Inside, it's the exact opposite of the outside. It's like a movie set in here. Tropical banana plants, palm trees, miniature tangerines, exotic purple orchids, caged parrots screaming their heads off, finches twittering. The fireplace and baseboard heat are cranked up so high the ceiling's dripping. Outside—just on the other side of the tall, doubled-paned bay windows—it's nine below zero and even though the gigantic sun will soon be blazing high over the frozen St. Croix River, the ice remains eighteen inches thick. Thick enough for employees of the Andersen Windows company to drive straight across it from Wisconsin to the Minnesota shore and save a half-hour's commuting time. At the crack of dawn you can watch them through these steaming windows starting out with their headlights gleaming, crawling along in weaving amber lines through the fishing huts and little square tents, smoke wisping out their vent pipes. Fishermen huddle inside these tents frying bacon and walleye, tossing back schnapps and listening to rabid talk radio throw opinions at them from a world far away. They're happy campers watching for the slightest twitch of fluorescent green bobbers. I don't get it myself. I was raised near the Mojave where we slept with the windows wide open and watched the distant foothills burn through the night.

Stillwater

The electronic chimes from the brick Lutheran church tower are playing "Onward, Christian Soldiers" with crisp mathematical precision in the chill morning air. The melody line pierces the windows of every house in the neighborhood. No one escapes. It is a spectacular, bright fall day in the St. Croix River Valley; powder blue skies, fluffy clouds, no wind to speak of. The kind of day, as they like to say up here, that is the reason they all suffer the most godawful winters on earth. It is also the fifth day in a row that bombs have been falling on distant Kabul and Kandahar.

The hardwoods along the banks of the Mississippi are blazing yellow and orange. Bald eagles and giant osprey cruise the inlets for walleye. In the distance, delicate sailboats and fishing skiffs ply the little harbor in silent slow motion. Everything here is quiet and peaceful beyond words:

> Onward, Christian soldiers, marching as to war
> with the cross of Jesus going on before

Dawson, Minnesota

(Highway 212 East)

Gnomes
and the Dead
and corn
and soybeans
and Cenex
and Gnomes
on the lawns
and the Dead laid out
and the corn
horizon to horizon
sea to shining sea

Demon in the Woods

Every evening this little yellow dog of mine comes rushing up to meet me; nervous, panting, turning in circles around my legs. I don't know what it's all about. It's as though she expects me to save her from some demon in the woods. I try to tell her I have no answers to it. No solution. I'm scared the same way myself, some-times. I don't know what about. There's something out there lurk-ing, though. No doubt about it. I can hear its fiery breath behind the old black locust. I can see it sometimes swooping through the fields. Sometimes it hovers right above me. I don't look up. I keep my eyes tight to the ground. Right in rhythm with my walking stick.

Gardening in the Dark

Weeding my garden in the pitch-black dark. In the cool of the night. And the mockingbird raving as though it were light. And the moaning train. And the cow calling and the calf answers back. And the candle hysterically beaten in the breeze.

It's all adding up.

Happy Man

These delicious mornings he takes his black coffee out on the stone porch and just sits in the old Adirondack chair, handmade in Wisconsin out of raw red cedar, water stains running down the wide flat arms. He just sits there sipping and listening to the mockingbird go through its wild variations; watches geese and canvasbacks winging down across the lower pasture; hears the long trucks moaning east and west on distant Highway 64. A woodpecker hammers away at the dead hackberry. His gray gelding comes trotting up the fence line snorting for carrots then walks off grazing through pink clover. He's a happy man. No question. The sun is pulling steam out of the ground all the way down to the river. The smell of rotting hay and mulch fills him. The giant irises he's planted are just beginning to explode into lavender and white plumes. A jeweled hummingbird travels down the whole line poking its head into each bearded bloom then just vanishes off into the woods. Red-winged blackbirds surround him, making their watery croak. His yellow dog sleeps on her side; stretched out across the flat river stones, soaking up the last coolness of morning through her flat ribs. The man lights a half-smoked cigar, sips his coffee, and cracks open *The Astonished Man*. He wants nothing more. He might just sit here all day, he thinks. He might just sit out here all year until the snow flies. Why not? What's to stop him?

Promising Two-Year-Old

The axiom goes: "No man with a promising two-year-old ever committed suicide."

He hangs on the training track rail at 4:00 a.m. in the pitch dark, feeling the rumble of hooves through the turn coming right up into the hollows of his old knees. He sips on his hot chocolate and coffee mix and feels like a genius for breeding this blistering-fast colt. The whole rest of his life is a catastrophe; his marriage, his family, his dying friends, his lost opportunities. But this colt—even in the dark, as he flashes by—rippling sorrel muscle—the rhythmic blasts from the nostrils—this colt lights up what's left of the man's mind. That part that still lies vulnerable to brilliance and courage. It lifts him up like a love affair or the great ball of sun just now cracking over the backstretch.

Mandan, North Dakota

(Highway 94)

First light. Outside the Super 8. Glass doors. Smell of weak coffee. Chattering of all the Mandan Indian cleaning ladies sitting on the curb of the parking lot like crows on a wire; giggling, hungover in red, white, and blue heart-patterned blouses. Uniforms issued by the motel, way too small for these women who like to eat. Belly rolls, flesh-colored bras, lacy black thongs can't hold back the blood of their ancient ancestors. They crouch, puffing away on Marlboro Lights, gulping down the delicious gray smoke. Behind them, stacked on aluminum wagons—clean white fluffy towels smelling like Tide, small bars of pink soap, rolls and rolls of toilet paper, waiting; the day's work in front of them.

Two hundred years ago on this very spot where the black parking lot sprawls out to the cottonwoods and these Mandan women nurse their hangovers, this is what Captain Meriwether Lewis jotted down in his notebook concerning a baby boy born to a Snake woman called Sacagawea:

"(February 11, 1805) . . . about five oclock this evening one of the wives of Charbono was delivered of a fine boy. it is worthy of remark that this was the first child which this woman had boarn and as is common in such cases her labour was tedious and the pain violent; Mr. Jessome informed me that he had freequently adminstered a small portion of the rattle of the rattlesnake, which he assured me had never failed to produce the desired effect, that of hastening the birth of the child; having the rattle of a snake by me I gave it to him and he administered two rings of it to the woman broken in small pieces with the fingers and added to a small quantity of water. Whether this medicine was truly the cause or not I shall not undertake to determine, but I was informed that she had not taken it more than ten minutes before she brought forth."

Miles City, Montana

(Highway 94 West)

Seven young firefighters from the BLM Forest Service are looking
for rooms in the War Bonnet Inn. I'm standing, waiting in line
right behind them in the lobby. Their exhausted faces; red eyes,
hooded in ash, the steel toes of their boots burned black. Montana's on fire. Miles of open rangeland in flames right up to the
shoulder of the interstate. That's all anyone talks about around
here. How to contain it. Where exactly the giant Caterpillars have
cut the breaks. How often the planes are bombing the wild ridges
with water canisters. How many new conflagrations have sponta-
neously erupted from Bozeman to Missoula and beyond; up into
the High Line, threatening the ski resorts from Kalispell to Hungry
Horse? Blame it on Big Bad Nature, touching down. Lightning
from the Thunder Gods. They're laughing at us from far away;
watching us scramble in earthly horror. As soon as one blaze gets
extinguished another flares up. We're chasing our tails down here.

By the time I step up to the desk all the rooms have been taken.
More long pickups loaded with young firefighters are pouring into
the parking lot as I come out of the lobby into the glowing red
dusk. The air smells strong of burning pine and sagebrush. Your
eyes sting of ash. Maybe Billings has a room. Down the burning
highway. Maybe Billings.

Wichita, Kansas

(Highway 35 North)

Whiteout in Wichita. Stuck down deep in ice and snow. Wind blowing sideways, slashing forty miles per hour. Traffic, dead-stopped, both ways; four lanes bumper to bumper, far as the eye can see. It's apocalyptic. People from all over America jumping out of their cars into twenty degrees, climbing up on their hoods try-ing to see what the holdup is. Nobody's dressed for the catastro-phe; some of them in pajamas, bellies hanging out, pants falling down their asses, knocking ice off the windshields, walking tiny shivering hairless dogs in doggy jackets. One guy gets out in blue sweatpants and a black T-shirt. Back of his shirt says in bold let-ters: "You may all go to Hell. I will go to Texas," signed—Davy Crockett. Thank God for Guy Clark on my satellite radio.

Valentine, Nebraska

(Highway 20)

Can't you just sit still? What's the matter with you, anyway? You're driving me nuts. All this constant moving around. Look at you. You're a mess. Even now your leg is jumping like a jackhammer. Your fingers are twitching. Your eyes, leaping all over the wallpaper. What's going on? You're not going to last very long if you keep this up, you know. You'll burn yourself out. Can't you just follow some sort of itinerary, at least? Some plan. What am I supposed to make of all this—all this crashing around? What in the world is so interesting about *not* having an objective? I mean, look at this map! Just take a look at it. You show up in Baton Rouge, then you're off to Saskatoon, then down to Butte; Mountain Home. Pendleton. It's insane. It makes no sense. How is anybody supposed to follow this? Look at these lines! These underlines. These pink, highlighted highways; roads I've never even heard of. Where in the hell is the "Little Dixie Highway," anyway? I, for one, am not tagging along anymore. I've had it. I can't keep up. My car can't take it. All the wear and tear. Four-dollar gas and we wind up in some pissant hellhole like Winnemucca or Cucamonga. I mean, what the fuck? What's the point? And what do we have to show for it after all these miles? A bunch of damn coffee mugs with place-name cafés. A buffalo paperweight. What's it all add up to? Nada, man. Absolutely nada. I've come to the end of the line. I really have. I realized that this morning. From now on you're on your own. I'm walking out the door. Don't try following me either because you'll never find me. Oh—and don't worry about the room. I got that covered. Least I can do after all we've been through. Are you listening to me? Do you understand what I'm saying! I'm walking out the fucking door! Right now. Adios! Here I go.

(Door slams. Silence. No movement of any kind.)

Is it actually true that Christopher Columbus gave false information to his sailors regarding the position of his ship so they couldn't find their way back, in the event of mutiny?

Devil's Music

(Montana, Highway 2)

From Culbertson to Cut Bank, all along the High Line, he ripped his voice out completely. At first he was just managing to sing along politely with the Howlin' Wolf Chess collection; dodging in and out of feeble harmony attempts on "Back Door Man" and "Moanin' at Midnight," but gradually he became carried away in a frenzy of exultation. By the time he hit Kalispell his throat was actually bleeding but he couldn't stop himself. Something had taken over. He kept desperately trying to find the shift from the high nasal megaphone pitch down into Wolf's deep growling groans of lost love and tortured treachery but he just couldn't find it. He was stuck somewhere smack in the middle. Torn apart. Truckers blew by him with American flags flapping from every possible fixture; staring down in bewilderment at his bloated purple face, screaming to the wind: "I asked her for water but she brought me gasoline!" He passed ranchers on three-wheelers gathering calves as he belched out "Smokestack Lightnin'," torturing himself with the failure to make the transition into the shaky howls and terrible haunting swings of Wolf's paranoia: "Don't you hear me crying?" "Where'd you sleep last night?" The sky dipped into great bars of plum-colored clouds as the sun set behind the Bitterroots and he pressed on hypnotically toward Bonners Ferry. He checked into the Motel 8 there but his voice wouldn't work at all. Nothing came out but a faint wheeze. He kept smiling apologetically to the little gray woman behind the desk and pushing his credit card toward her so at least she'd know he was good for the rent. He took the Wolf CD with him into room #6, on the ground floor, but there was nothing to play it on so he sat on the edge of the bed and read the liner notes: How Wolf ended up weeping for his mother on his deathbed but she never came to visit. She had forsaken him a long time ago for singing the Devil's music.

I can make a deal

I can make a deal with myself
for maybe a day
say
maybe two
some kind of clean trade-off
swap

back on track
morning line
banish the haunted hooch

I can make a deal

I can make a deal till the sun goes down
then the whole thing's off
terminado
finito
out de door

I'm just not sure anymore
I can handle total oblivion
without some sauce

Butte, Montana

Richard Hugo's astoundingly American poem, "Degrees of Gray in Philipsburg," keeps coursing through my head up here, in this grim brick mining town:

You might come here Sunday on a whim.
Say your life broke down.

Roofs keep blowing off the meth-lab shacks sitting directly across the street from neat little Scandinavian bungalows, geranium flower boxes in the windows. Chemical explosions out of nowhere. Shirtless rapists, spiderwebs tattooed across their faces, sift through the wreckage; appearing and disappearing in black smoke. This is the childhood home of Evel Knievel and his "Days" are here; streets thronged with bikers, everyone cruising for a fight. Cops tell me someone's always trying to grab their guns away from them every time they walk into a bar. Kid was killed just last night, down at the Wagon Wheel. Someone smashed his head against a toilet bowl, ran out laughing.

Back at the turn of some century, Carry Nation, the temperance reformer famous for her hatchet-wielding saloon smashing, made a pilgrimage to Butte. She was beaten to a bloody pulp by one of the whorehouse madams for trying to convert her clientele. Carry died on an eastbound train, heading back to civilization; bleeding to death from her wounds. Sitting directly across from her on the hard oak seats was a U.S. marshal; twelve-gauge propped on his hip, ramrod straight and unsmiling. Beside him were four renegade Cheyenne chained together by their ankles and wrists. The warrior right next to the marshal had an iron necklace and a wide black stripe running down his forehead and nose, across his lips to the chin. His black eyes cut through Carry's. He and the marshal stared straight across at her as she slowly bled to death. They watched her very closely, like they would a dying sparrow.

get out of Butte altogether
why pretend to get along here
get on up to Missoula at least
just do me a favor and
get the fuck out of Butte
poison red ruby lake
crackhead air
roofs blowing sky high
how many signs do you need
one dumb little joint that sells organic bread
salty pumpkin seeds in a coffee can
like as though they were going to philosophically save this town
from suicide and mutilation
just get out
blow on across the Little Blackfoot
phosphate and Philipsburg
make tracks for rosy Cutthroat
three-pound Browns
get it completely out of your head
that you'll ever settle in
warm and toasty
with a dog that never sheds
and a big-hipped woman
who thinks the sun rises and sets
on your miserable toothless head

Ft. Robinson, Nebraska

(Highway 20)

I pick up this common gray stone on the spot where Crazy Horse was killed; September 5, 1877. It looks a little like a hawk's beak with a dark crooked ridge running across the back. It's hot from lying out flat in the sun for who knows how long. No telling if it might have been kicking around back then; a dumb witness to the outrageous murder. Catholics might call this stone a "second-class relic," since there's no proof of its origins, only the association with the place. I drop it deep in my pocket, on top of my black jackknife. It's warm down there. Who knows if it holds any power. I guess we'll find out somewhere down the road.

I am crying in my heart, after the manner of white men.
                                                —KIT CARSON

Wounded Knee,
Pine Ridge Reservation

The large metal sign on the dusty shoulder of Highway 27, explaining, front and back, the horrific events that took place here in December 1890, has been altered. The word *battle* has been covered over with a patchwork metal plate riveted to the sunbleached narrative reading *massacre* in bold black letters. "Massacre" replaces "battle," as if that's all the correction we need to alter our thinking about it. As if now we are able to digest the actuality of carnage, one hundred and twenty years in our past.

Pathetic little lean-tos roofed with pine boughs shelter wrinkled-up Lakota women selling beaded crafts and crude jewelry. It's 103 degrees and the wind is swirling across the broken highway sending up dust devils. White plastic coffee cups and potato chip bags go whipping by. A dark hawk high above a field of burnt grass tumbles and swoops through the hot-air currents, hoping for some sign of varmints below. I decide to park beside a line of glittering Harleys directly across the highway from the monument; thinking that driving up the hill to the sight might be disrespectful. There's also some nagging notion that walking up the hill in this sledgehammer heat might be some slight form of penance. (I don't know where these notions of guilt originate.) I'm staring down at my boots in the powdery clay as I climb toward the two brick columns, arched by a steel span with a small cross in the middle. "Walking through time," I whisper. I reach the top and pull out my disposable Kodak that I've been using to record catch-and-release Rainbows. I've only got a couple shots left. As I'm trying to focus on the raggedy monument, a boy's face jumps into the frame then darts back out. A skinny teenage Lakota boy with wide eyes and a crooked smile. He peeks out at me from behind one of the brick columns. I take my eye away from the lens and see two more boys hiding behind the structures. I call out to them and ask if I can take their picture in front of the monument. They shyly reveal themselves, barefoot in grimy T-shirts, clutching aluminum cans of Pepsi. I ask if they can bunch together under the steel arch. They giggle and line up facing me then, suddenly, as I raise the Kodak to my eye, they all throw their fists to the sky mimicking the Black Panther salute of the sixties. I have no idea what era I'm living in.

Rosebud, South Dakota

(Highway 83 North)

Shitty little government A-frames spit out across the Sandhills. Not a human in sight. Just evidence: Ripe garbage piled high. Bullet holes in every window. Flapping black plastic. Three-quarter ply nailed across the doors like hurricane protection but there's only an ocean of sand. Wailing. You can hear its constant moan. Yellow sunburned sandbox slides. Bright red plastic swings. No kids to speak of. Backyards way too far from the house. Prairie swallows them all up. Lakota church, "Open to Anyone," it says, but no one's here. Not a single sorry soul. And it's the Sabbath too. Imagine that. Sunday abandoned. Just constant wind ripping across the tattered yards and buried fences. Constant endless prairie breath. Like it's always been. Now and evermore. Unrelenting. Raw. And could care less about the state of the Union.

I thought there was a hawk
sitting at the bar
above the beer
gazing out
as though from the top of a hickory fencepost
indifferent
back to me
shoulders humped like some old Ute
but no
it was only me
tripping again
on roads
long past
roads
I'd slammed the hammer down
one too many times

Mojado

Today, I feel exactly like a dark mojado on a freeway overpass. Black pack on my back, staring out over the streaming traffic; cars pouring under my wide blistered feet.

I'm turning slowly in one place, looking for some sign; some familiar tree, some rock. I'm turning full circle but nothing speaks to me.

Today, I feel exactly like this short Sonoran man searching for some distant cousin he's never met. They promised he'd be here with a job, cold cerveza, and tennis shoes. But he's nowhere to be found. He's nowhere around.

Normal

(Highway 39 South)

Under the blaring neon of the drunk-tank lockup he studied the cinder-block walls. There was nothing much else to do. Arms slack between knees. Knees folded up to accommodate the short length of the cot. A weird light green plastic burlap-sack-type of mattress propped under his head. Remarkable absence of graffiti, he thought to himself as he scanned the contours. Someone had attempted some desperate scrapings on the steel frame of the window but there were no letters; no words of any kind. Not even a lover's name or a racial slur. No pictographs of genitalia even. Just random gashes into the steel. He wondered what type of sharp object could have been used since all personal possessions are confiscated long before they slam the door on you. Maybe a zipper. But how would anyone manage to get their crotch up that high to the window frame without being spotted through the thick glass by one of the zealous young officers in crew cuts. Whoever it was would have had to drop their jeans, he figured; stand on the rough ledge of the cot, pants in hand, and scrape away in fits and flurries, ducking frantically each time someone came patrolling down the corridor. Must have been a young man, he thought. Young, scared, and angry. Full of rage. He no longer had it in him, he realized. The fight. The hate. The energy. That was mainly it. Just exhaustion and dismay. He panned the walls, searching for some recognizable symbol of civilization. A crude five-pointed star fashioned with intersecting lines but not overtly Jewish. More like a token of achievement a fourth-grade teacher might scribble in the margin of your notebook. Next to it, a tall number 15 gashed at an angle with the tail of the 5 trailing off into a tropical bird feather. Beautiful but unintended. Beauty seemed more and more like that these days. Accidental. Miraculous, maybe. He kept scanning: another tangle of slashes that he read anthropomorphically into a stick-figure man with an oversize head, wielding an ax. It could have easily been something depicted on the ancient cave walls of France. A giant stag crashing to earth. Fires in the vast blackness. Log drums through the endless woods.

.　　.　　.　　.　　.

So
fact is
they ask me
who can you get
to wire you a hundred and fifty bucks
you need a hundred and fifty more
to complete your bond

I was at a loss
I said no one
no one
they said back
that's right I said
come on they said
you must have someone out there
no I said
there's no one

they must have thought I was lying
so they threw me in here
slammed the door

> never even tried the knob
> I knew it was curtains
> I'm not in here for lying
> I know that much
> I'm in here for blowing
> twice the state limit

. . . . .

Guy in the cell next door is shrieking like a beagle in heat. He deliberately bashed his head against the wall when they tossed him in there. Spotted blood all over the floor, like red cottage cheese. I saw it as they walked me past there, handcuffed. Officer grumbled he wasn't cleaning it up. The mess. Idiot smashed his own damn head. Idiot could damn sure clean it up. Or sleep in it. Which was what he was doing.

Now these raw wall scrapings are starting to move all by themselves. Flicker and dance. I remember reading somewhere they burned Jean Genet's manuscript of *Our Lady of the Flowers* when they discovered it hidden in his cell. He then proceeded to write the whole thing over again—on toilet paper.

. . . . .

> Where have they taken my Chevy
> I wonder
> Will I ever see my white Chevy again

Elkhorn River

I'm in the Elkhorn up to my knees. My yellow dog floats past, hunting crawdads; her black eyes flat and darting on top of her head, like some wild fat opossum. Managed to catch three green smallmouth so far in the same deep hole. I've stopped counting the snags I've had on mossy rock and sunken sycamore. At least no thorny thoughts so far. No haunted memories. Just red-winged-blackbird songs and honking geese. Around the river bend, toward the old bridge I can hear Mexican voices getting closer. Splashing, laughing. Men and boys. Jokes. Tales of chicas way back in some jungle village. Here they come, around the turn; men and sons, crashing right up the middle, casting wide nets in white spiraling fans, like they must have always done in their Caribbean home-land. Spanish shrieks through the thick Kentucky air. Birds and squirrels dash for cover. Silver fish and crawdads spill through mestizo fingers as this little tribe goes wading right past me, pressing upriver; roaring with their brotherhood.

How is it I got cast out here so far in this Kentucky wilderness? Was it horses or women? How did it come to pass that Mayan men are more a part of these snaking waters than my white flat feet touching bottom?

Horse

Dragging my dead gelding by tractor on a chain down to the deep ditch, crying like a baby. Thank God there's no one on the farm right now. Just dogs, chickens, and cattle. Thank God for that. No one to see me like this, all grimaced up in grief; doubled over just about. The head of the horse bumping along over gravel and thick weeds; muscles of the neck flowing with every contour of land— flowing for the last time as they already begin to lock up. This great old gelding; son of Peppy San Badger, blood of King Ranch, carried me into the herd so many times; paralyzed cattle with his stare, rattled the bit in the ground. Now he's going down in a black hole. Thank God there's no one on the farm right now. Just dogs, chickens, cattle, and me.

Descendancy

Here I am again in the bright white glare of fluorescent tubes framing the cheap mirror of a two-banger motor home parked off Paseo de Peralta in the very town where my dad lies buried and my daughter was born. Here I am yet again in another movie, at my age, playing yet another military man, which I'm not and never will be but my father most certainly was and all his brothers and their father and grandfather and great-grandfather going back to the fall of Richmond and further back to Concord and Lexington and back some more to the Norman Invasion and pagans wearing calf skulls and Viking invasions and burials in longboats with dragon-headed prows. I don't know how far back you want to carry this thing. What's the point? Who are you hoping to find back there, anyhow? Some seer? Some diviner of destinies? And here they come again now, calling me on their walkie-talkies; banging politely on my metal door: ADs, Assistant ADs, assistants to the assistants of ADs. Making sure I'm ready. Suited up. Making sure I'm ready to be ready, just in case they're ready. Any second now they might need me to step in front of the camera and portray this ongoing character in a decorated uniform with an aura of tired, grim determination in the face of hopeless odds. Where did I ever come up with an affinity for such a character, such a man? The arrogant jut of the jaw. The downcast scowl. And this terrible sense of impending doom? Was it from as far back as the steel seat of a

Day out of Days

Jeep in the Mariana Islands sitting beside my mother in monsoon rain? Was it in the back of my father's neck where he picked compulsively at his shrapnel scars? Or is it somewhere deep inside the terror of being lost in the Great Basin at night with no lights and you've run completely out of gas? No use fishing in the dark. Put your costume on. Walk out there and face the music. Hopefully, some mask will appear. Someone from long ago, I might recognize. Something that might just tap me on the shoulder and invite me out of here. Believe me, I wouldn't hesitate.

Durango, Mexico

He drives me out here to location. He won't let *me* drive. It's a matter of pride or union orders, I guess. I'm his guest, he says, and then he's silent for miles. I don't speak much Spanish so he stays silent. I can't blame him. When I speak English he smiles and nods politely; relieved. I don't know how much he understands. The miles click by. When I speak my stumbling Spanish a dark cloud crosses his face and a look of deep pity casts into his Indian eyes as though I were a "pobrecito"—one of the slab-sided dogs we go flying by; splashing mud on white sows and squealing gilts. We flash past stake trucks, broke down in the lava rocks, stacked high with sweet pine logs, flocks and flocks of swirling cowbirds like falling decks of cards. We head out into the pink Sierras in his beat to shit Oldsmobile, fenders flapping, and leave Mesquitillo's bare dirt streets in the dust. The only car we pass is wheelless; jacked way up on wood Modelo crates. Naked two-year-olds peek out at us from behind fresh sheets, blowing in the high mountain air. The viejos here say they still remember Pancho Villa crashing through this very town on a plain bay horse; galloping toward a historical moment which he entirely staged for the American cameras. Clever bastard.

Tulum, Mexico

Early morning, the little Mayan man rakes the white sand in beautiful crosshatched strokes like a woven basket. He takes such great care with it you wonder what ancient sect of craftsmen passed this impulse down to him. He piles the seaweed and chunks of ragged plastic blown in from Cuba into neat little stacks then collects them all with a wooden wheelbarrow. His feet are wide and leathery like something from Diego Rivera.

Slowly, the tourists begin to emerge from their pink cabanas hauling rubber rafts and tall mixed drinks down to the surf. They set themselves up in distinct camps, depending on language and culture. Some drop their tops. Others stay buttoned up clear to the neck. One of them is peeling badly and her husband slathers heavy-duty sunblock all over her back. She winces at his every touch.

On the edge of the coconut palm grove a buxom Mexican woman lurks in the stripes of shade. She's scanning the tourists with wild eyes, searching for any vulnerable single man. She reminds me of that fat woman from Fellini's *Amarcord* who seduced all the young boys on the beach. What was her name? Serafina, maybe? She spots a ripe victim and approaches him quickly, almost tiptoeing through the crosshatch marks left by the little Mayan man. She asks the startled tourist, who is reading a Graham Greene novel, if he would like to go with her into the palm grove and get a deep massage. He shakes his head vehemently and rolls over on his belly, shocked at the interruption. One of the waiters from the resort spots the buxom woman and comes running at her, frantically waving a white linen napkin. He chases her off, back into the slender palms, as though she were a pesky seabird. Their tracks have ripped a violent swath through the perfect basket-weave. The waiter apologetically returns to the man reading the Graham Greene novel just as his slinky girlfriend heads toward him in a glistening purple bikini, carrying the *New York Times*. Little puffs of sand punctuate her every step. The waiter backs off, bowing and scraping. The buxom woman is still lurking, watching it all from a distance.

Boca Paila, Mexico

Why would he ever think, on arriving at midnight through sand and dank luggage, morning might miraculously bring some bright new shining faces to the plank breakfast table from as far away as Omaha, say, or maybe Saskatchewan, Tonopah, Del Rio? Is he finally getting that desperate for company?

Must be all the white identical rental cars jammed up against the blowing palms; the crashing Caribbean repeating the same old song he's just now beginning to recognize.

Why would he ever think he'd become truly engaged talking "issues" with strangers when all they ever do is divide and separate along lines that real fishermen come here to get away from anyway? He would most likely draw a dead blank on every one and create a deep dark paranoia over the pineapple and cantaloupe.

Anyhow, it's clear they're only here for the disposable photograph with some stunned world record Tarpon, a giant Jack or Permit. One of the bigger fellas obviously works for the Secret Service, although he thinks he's anonymous. You can tell by his shaved neck, the automatic bulge in his Simms vest, and the puff in his concave chest.

The top-heavy wives hang behind on the beach, reading historical novels and spine-tingling Grisham under lime green umbrellas. They've left nothing behind.

Just lying here listening to my daughter smash mosquitoes in the next room; smacking her thigh. The waves are softer tonight; lapping almost. Wind has died down. Someone is playing repetitive Euro-disco nowhere music next door. All I can make out is the deadening bass line. My daughter's mosquito smashing grows louder and more violent. Her torture is palpable. Her mother rolls over right beside me and yells out: "You can't just slash away at mosquitoes! You have to be precise!" Her voice carries the authority of the Minnesota Boundary Waters. The smashing from my daughter's room stops. Her candle goes out.

Quintana Roo, Mexico

Finally, the blind man and his companion sit down right next to me on the beach. I've been curious about them for days and now, here they are suddenly. It seems odd they should be so close up when I've been observing them always from a distance; watching how the shorter man gently leads the blind man into the surf by the elbow then lets go of him once the waves begin to crash around their knees. They just stand there staring across in the direction of Hispaniola. Now, they turn and cross the white sand up the hill, back toward the restaurant; the blind man always behind holding onto the shorter man's flowered shirt, very softly. Nothing desperate. Nothing urgent. I follow them and sit down directly across at a round table. I can't help staring straight into the blind man's eyes. He never wears dark glasses and his eyes are wide open, unblinking. They're obviously synthetic eyes, like two large olives in a pale martini. I can see that these synthetic eyes are definitely not seeing mine. I look away quickly toward the green sea when his companion notices me staring. Far offshore the surf is breaking across the coral reef in a thin white line. The frigate bird soars high above, wings unmoving. What a creation.

Dogs really know how to run down here. Away from gasoline-driven demons. Maniacs on bikes. Still, the movement never stops. The night. Squealing, flat-bellied girls on their purple spangled cell phones. Screaming with delight. Disfigured dolls hanging off the hitches of pickup trucks. And always the overripe pregnant ones from out of the skinny alleys, babies in each hand, ice cream running down their arms. Behind them, in a grass palapa, something's being sacrificed to the Gods of Wind. Maybe it's a new white goat brought down from Mérida. Maybe it's something from an entirely different time. Only one thing's certain. It never stops.

Land of the Living

"It's just amazing how friendly you become when you're on Zenax," she says. This is after we've been standing in the long snaking customs line for over an hour in the torrid Cancún heat. We're being herded, shoulder to shoulder, with all the other Minnesota "snowbirds" frantically fanning themselves with their immigration forms.

"I know," I say to her. "I'm amazed myself."

"*You're* amazed?"

"Yes, I am."

"Why should you be amazed?"

"Well, I feel this friendly person coming out in me and I wonder if maybe that's my real nature. You know—the real me."

"Well, what is it that's changed exactly?"

"I'm on Zenax."

"I understand that," she says. "But what is it that makes you more friendly than before you took the Zenax?"

"Well, I'm not a particularly *unfriendly* person, am I?"

"Not now, you're not."

"No, I mean, I don't ordinarily think of myself as a sullen, bad-tempered kind of a guy."

"I didn't say sullen."

"Well—"

"You don't usually go out of your way to be chatty. Let's put it that way."

"Chatty?"

"You're chatting about the weather with total strangers. You never do that. Not as long as I've known you."

"Well, I thought it was kind of remarkable, don't you?"

"What?" she says.

"The weather. The change. The extreme difference between here and St. Paul in a matter of just three and a half hours."

"That's why people come here from St. Paul. The change in the weather. That's why *we're* here."

"Yes, I know that, but it's still remarkable, isn't it? A hundred and five here and minus thirty back there."

"Never mind," she says, and turns toward the slow-motion overhead fan.

There's a group of elementary-school teachers from Duluth right in front of us who suddenly burst into singing "When the Bear Comes over the Mountain" in perfect unison with no attempt at harmony. I guess the pulverizing heat and the waiting have tipped them right over the edge. The Mexican officials in SWAT Team uniforms look on in stony silence, arms clasped behind their backs, black Mayan eyes unmoved by this Nordic display of bravado. Our teenage kids have slumped completely to the concrete floor, heads propped on their backpacks, surrendered to the heat. They've stopped volunteering any conversation.

"Actually, I'm just glad to be alive," I blurt out after standing there awhile in a kind of stupor, hypnotized by the schoolteachers' ditty.

"You're glad to be alive?" she repeats in astonishment. "Is that what you just said?"

"Yes, I am. Just like Arnold Palmer."

"Arnold Palmer?"

"Isn't that what he says these days? Now that he's ancient; hobbling down the fairway. 'I'm just glad to be here. Just glad to be alive.' That's what he says when they run up to him with microphones and TV cameras, you know, for those golf show interviews. Even when he's having trouble with his putting, his swing. Isn't that what he always says now?"

"I have no idea. I thought he was dead."

"Arnold Palmer? No. He's very much alive. He's an icon."

"Whatever," she says and turns away again.

"Well, it's true," I continue. "I'm thrilled to still be here; back in the 'land of the living.' "

"I didn't realize you'd left us," she says.

"Well, that's the way I always feel when I've survived an airplane trip."

"Survived?"

"I always feel like I'm actually going to die when I get on an airplane. Like this is it, the end of the line; inevitable. Then, after we land and get back on dry land it feels as though I've lived through a kind of certain death and come out the other end. That's why I take Zenax and that's why I say I'm glad to be alive." She stares at me a second in absolute bewilderment, as though she's looking into the face of a total stranger, then turns back to the long stale line of humans in limbo.

"My God," she says. "What is taking so long with this customs thing? We've never had to wait this long before. What the hell is going on?" Just beyond the singing schoolteachers (who've now taken to doing the song in rounds, like Campfire Girls) is a somber couple I recognize from the Lindbergh Airport back in St. Paul. The man: in a wheelchair, somewhat older than the woman; late fifties maybe, blanket across his lap, a plaid scarf around his neck in spite of the stifling heat, and an odd alpine-style hat with a little brush sticking out of the band. The woman (his wife?) stands behind him, very erect, hands propped at the ready on the gray grips of the wheelchair, as though assigned to a permanent grim vigil. She is plainly pretty in a Midwestern open-faced, innocent way; wearing a light linen suit and white pumps—not exactly the expected attire for Yucatán beach life. The two of them seem completely detached from the goings-on: the silly singing; the constant fanning of everyone around them which has now become some kind of communal gesture of contempt for the Mexican bureaucracy. Nothing seems to ruffle the couple's deep stoicism. Now and then, the woman slips a white handkerchief from her pocket and gently daubs the man's forehead and the corners of his mouth, although I can't make out any moisture. He doesn't seem to be suffering the consequences of a stroke or neurological disorder but rather a much longer and slower debilitation. Whatever it is, it's clearly taken its toll on the two of them.

Now, finally, the line begins to trickle forward. We prod our kids up off the floor and shove the luggage down through the roped-off alley-maze toward the customs inspectors. The abrupt, unexpected flow of the line seems to have caught the schoolteachers up short. They're scrambling for their baggage. The austere couple rolls silently on. The man's pale head slowly tilts upward, drawn by the tropical sunlight blasting through the tall arched windows of the main terminal. Each window frames an absolutely motionless palm tree outside. Heat waves brand themselves across the glass in vapored sheets. A single green parrot desperately wings its way from one palm to the next as though he might not make it; as though the savage heat might drop him flat in midflight.

•　•　•　•　•

We find ourselves crammed into a red Jeep Wrangler with a flapping canvas top. (The much larger Chevy Suburban I'd reserved having been let go due to our delay in the customs line. Mexico waits for no man.) My son immediately drops off to sleep, his six-foot-plus rail-thin frame crunched up in back with the luggage. Our daughter leans her head against the pipe roll bar, a T-shirt wedged between the steel and her soft temple. Thick jungle air pours across her face. My wife has gone completely silent now, staring up at a gigantic billboard of nearly naked brown twins coyly concealing their perfect breasts behind icy bottles of Corona. "Have you got a girlfriend?" she asks me out of the blue.

"A girlfriend?" I say, checking to see if our daughter may have overheard this but she too has been put to sleep by the heat.

"Yes, that's right. A girlfriend," my wife repeats.

"Where did this come from?"

"Don't act so surprised. You could very easily have a girlfriend and I'd never know it, would I? How would I know?"

"I'm sixty. Those days are over."

"Lots of young women are attracted to that these days. It's become chic or something."

"Attracted to what?"

"Older men. Men of influence."

"Men of influence?"

"Don't laugh. You know what I'm talking about."

"No, I don't have a girlfriend."

"How did I know you were going to say exactly that?" She stifles a little giggle, biting her lower lip.

"Could we talk about this later?" I suggest quietly.

"When?" she says.

"When we're not on vacation. When we're not riding down the Yucatán Peninsula with our children directly behind us."

"You do, don't you?" She smiles slowly at me with a look of supreme recognition then turns away toward the flying jungle. We pass a broken-down rock corral with ribby horses nosing through dust and their own manure. Blue patches of bottle flies blanket their eyes.

"Does this mean we're going to be silent and sour the whole rest of the trip?" I ask the back of her neck.

"We can be any way you want," she says without turning.

"Where in the world did this idea come from, anyway?"

"What idea?" she says.

"The idea that I have a girlfriend."

"It came from your cell phone, actually."

"My cell phone?"

"Yeah, that's right."

"*My* cell phone?"

"Are you going to just keep repeating yourself?"

"I'm repeating you."

"Yes, goddamnit, it came from your cell phone!" she bursts out. Both kids shift and grumble but never open their eyes.

"Could we talk about this later?" I say.

"That's something you said before too."

"I'm serious."

"I don't want to talk about it at all, actually. It's ridiculous. There's nothing to talk about anyway," she says with finality.

"So, you're just going to go ahead and believe in some crazy fantasy, some half-baked notion that popped into your head? Is that it?"

"It didn't 'pop' into my head, it came over your cell phone."

"What did?"

"A woman's voice."

"Oh—well, did you ask who it was? It could've been someone at the office."

"It wasn't 'someone at the office.' I'm familiar with everyone at the office and this wasn't one of them."

"It could've been anyone."

"Oh, please—"

"Well, it could've."

"All right, sure—yeah—right—it could've been anyone in the whole wide world, but it wasn't."

"I'm just saying—"

"Oh, shut up!" she suddenly shrieks. Our son wakes up with a jolt and snatches hold of the roll bar, waking his sister.

"What's wrong?" he pants, with his eyes popped out toward the road.

"Nothing," I say, "nothing. Just go back to sleep."

"What were you yelling about, Mom?" our daughter asks.

"I was yelling at your father."

"How come?"

"Because he's trying to deny he has a girlfriend and I've found out he has a girlfriend. Now go back to sleep."

"Great. That's really great," I say to my wife. "Congratulations."

"You're welcome," she says, and turns her entire back to me now.

Silence, except for the droning of the Jeep's oversize tires and the relentless jungle wind bashing the canvas top. The kids have burrowed back down into the luggage and returned to sleep. Her back is perfectly expressing expulsion. Exiled in the Yucatán.

"I might just as well have come down here all by myself," I say to her spine. No answer. We roar past Playa. Miles of fiesta-colored hammocks hanging in the heat; giant ochre pottery in the shapes of Mayan demons and once-sacred jungle creatures; jaguars, serpents, eagles, frogs. Everything's for sale on the carretera: rugs, serapes, Day-Glo wall hangings with lurid Aztec macho scenes; feathered warriors valiantly protecting young maidens from jade-eyed panthers. Huge billboards welcome us to the "Mayan Riviera" in English, as though Mexico were embarrassed to be Mexican. "I realize what it is now," I say out loud to myself but hoping she'll somehow respond. She doesn't. Her back remains a rigid blockade. The verdant jungle keeps rushing past. Now and then, a gap in the dense foliage. Daylight cracks through the tangle of vines and Chichin. Fleeting glimpse of an old man with his burro laden down with plastic milk containers filled from some secret cenote. Old sense of parallel lives. Separate. Haunted. I stumble on, just going on desperation now more than anything: "I think I realize now, what it is about the Zenax; how come I get so friendly on it." (I'm talking entirely to myself. The kids are snoring loudly.) "It's like with jazz musicians," I continue. "I remember all those guys down at the Five Spot in the sixties. They were all using smack back then. That was the drug of choice. I asked a drummer once why he was using it, and you know what he said?" (I don't know why I'm making a question out of this. Nobody's home. I soldier on.) "He told me he used it because it stopped all the inner chatter in his head. Isn't that amazing? It created a silence and then he could play."

For miles nothing happens. The mind goes on doing cart-wheels; shuffling through its files, rewriting the past then tripping on some little tidbit of what it calls reason: "What were you doing answering my cell phone, anyway? I don't answer your cell phone, do I?"

"Because it was ringing," she says out of nowhere.

"I thought you were asleep."

"I'm not."

"I thought you were pretending to be asleep."

"I'm not pretending anything," she says, still offering only her flat back.

"So, my cell phone was ringing and you picked it up—"

"It was ringing its fool head off; doing that dumb riff from 'Purple Rain' or whatever it is, jumping around on the bed. I only picked it up to stop the stupid ringing and jumping."

"And who answered?"

"You're asking *me*?" she says. Like an apparition, an old bare-foot Indian woman with a stack of firewood stands hunched over by the side of the road, waiting to cross six lanes of menacing traf-fic. Trucks shriek past her in both directions. It looks like she's been waiting there for hours. Dusk is descending through the bands of heat and all the great-tailed grackles are gathering in the locust trees.

. . . . .

By the time we reach the tiny resort in the pitch-black night I'm convinced that my life has now been capsized completely. I am worse than alone. I am a man traveling with bitter enemies who happen to be his most intimate family. It's become Greek or something worse. A roly-poly concierge emerges from an archway of bougainvillea, pushing a wheelbarrow and clenching a flashlight between his teeth. He's very glad to see us he says, once he's spit the flashlight out; his warm smile landing on our sorry faces. He informs us that the owners have gone to bed. They had stayed up, waiting for us, but it got too late. He has the key, though, and will show us to our room. He stacks our luggage on the wheelbarrow, bites down on the flashlight again, and we all follow him down the twisting stone path. Tall wind generators on metal poles are humming and flapping like exotic birds. The constant wind off the Caribbean is tearing at the palms, forcing them into a savage dance. I have this strange wish as we follow the bobbing beam of the flashlight, that we were all different people; strangers just happening to come together in the night. How much happier we might be if we didn't know each other at all. No history. No remorse.

. . . . .

Daybreak. The wind has calmed and the sea is flat and smooth clear to the horizon. The giant red sun presses up against the distant arc of the earth. How far away is the rest of the world? I'm the first one awake and happy to be alone on the beach. Tiny white crabs skitter into their holes at my approach. A string of sandpipers hurries ahead of me, darting in and out of the quiet surf. Above, the frigate bird soars. Turning back in the direction of the ancient Mayan ruins I see the couple from St. Paul, staring out silently at the rising sun; the woman holding her vigil behind the wheelchair exactly as she had at the airport. The man, in dark glasses, sits erect with his hat in his lap, both hands holding the brim. As the monster sun mounts the couple turns rosy red then slowly bright orange, as though they might suddenly burst into flame then crumble in ash to the sand. Neither of them moves an inch; frozen in the burning light. They have finally arrived.

My daughter slips up beside me, still half asleep, in sweatpants and a T-shirt with Bob Marley's face screaming across her chest. "Hi, Dad. I've never seen the sun so red as that, have you?"

"Only down here. I guess we must be closer to it or something. The Equator. Is that it?"

"Yeah, I guess. Did you have breakfast yet?"

"Nope. I don't even know if the kitchen's open yet."

"I thought I heard plates clanking up there."

"That's always a good sign," I say, giving her a kiss on the forehead. A slight talcum powder smell I remember from her as a baby goes dashing through me. Pure sweetness in the midst of this heartbreak. She takes my arm and we head off through the white sand toward the dining room. I take a short look back over my shoulder but the couple from St. Paul has vanished. I stop and turn around to scan the beach for them.

"What's the matter, Dad?"

"I don't know, I just saw those people down on the beach and now they're gone."

"What people?"

"That couple that was standing in line with us back at the airport. You probably didn't notice them."

"I was sleeping."

"Yeah. They just disappeared. How could that be?"

"I don't know. I'm hungry, aren't you?"

·　·　·　·　·

The tables in the dining room are all set with pink napkins and bright sprigs of bougainvillea propped in skinny glass vases. A Mayan waiter is pouring ice water from a metal pitcher. We sit by the window across from a pair of women dressed exactly alike in white starched shirts, red ties, and boyish haircuts. They hold hands across the table and stare out at the crashing surf. New Wave computer music is playing in hypnotic repetition like massage parlor background atmosphere. It gives the room a gloomy apocalyptic air. Nobody's smiling. The spectacular view of the white beach stretches clear down the narrow peninsula evaporating into billowy sea foam. Two dark soldiers emerge, strolling casually along the surf line, their hawklike Indian faces set hard against camouflage uniforms, black machine guns strapped to their backs. A fleet of white pelicans sails past them then dips low to the water. One of them plunges headlong into the green tide and comes up spewing mullet. "I just want you to know something, Emma," I say to my daughter as I smooth the pink napkin on my knee. "Your mother has no idea what she's talking about."

"What do you mean?" she says.

"Yesterday, in the car."

"What'd she say?"

"About— Didn't you hear what she was telling you?"

"Oh, about the girlfriend, you mean?"

"Yes."

"What about it?"

"Well—it's not true. It's a complete fabrication. I mean—my cell phone happened to be ringing and she picked it up and—"

"I really don't want to hear about it, Dad," she says, squeezing a wedge of lime onto her melon. "That's between you and her."

"Who? Me and who?"

"Mom. Who else?"

"Well, there's just no truth to it at all, is what I'm trying to say."

"It doesn't matter. It's got nothing to do with me."

234

"Well, it does, Emma. You're part of this family. I just don't want there to be some weird misunderstanding going on."

"There's no misunderstanding," she says and smiles across the table to the pair of women, still holding hands.

"I just don't know where she comes up with this stuff, tell you the truth. I mean, out of nowhere she makes this wild accusation. It's just—"

"Can we talk about something else, Dad? I mean, we're on vacation."

"Sure," I say and stare down into the swirling cloud of cream in my coffee.

A man with a goatee and Leicas strapped around his neck enters the dining room with two statuesque models. They stand aloof, meeting nobody's eyes; scanning the tables for a strategic location. The man raises his index finger to the waiter and points to a corner table, away from the direct sun. The waiter nods and offers a little half-bow. The models glide with a studied cadence as though every gesture were being played out for a spellbound audience.

"Are you getting excited about college?" I ask my daughter after a long pause.

"Yes," she says. "I am."

"Have you thought about what you're going to take?"

"Environmental studies, I think. There's also a class on women in the Civil War."

"That ought to be interesting. Which women? Do you mean famous women or—"

"Harriet Beecher Stowe, Mary Todd Lincoln. Women like that."

"Right," I say. "Mary Todd went nuts, didn't she?"

"Did she?"

"I think she did. After the assassination. Went into seclusion. Talked to herself—"

"Really?" my daughter says.

"I think so."

"Is that a sign of insanity?"

"What?"

"Talking to yourself?"

"Well—"

"Because I talk to myself all the time."

"You do?" I say.

"Well—not *all* the time."

"Sure. I mean, no—we all talk to ourselves *some* of the time."

"Do you talk to yourself?" she asks.

"Sure. I mean—now and then."

"What do you talk about? With yourself."

"Well—nothing, really."

"Nothing?"

"No—just little questions. Little—"

"Like what?" she says.

"Like—where did you leave your glasses, now? Or—"

"Oh, yeah, but that's just asking yourself something out loud. Everybody does that. But, I mean do you carry on long dialogues and have arguments with yourself? Stuff like that?"

"Arguments?" I say.

"Yes."

"No, do you?"

"Not really."

"Good. I'm glad to hear that. You had me worried there for a second." My daughter smiles and plops a chunk of pineapple into her mouth. "Well, that all sounds really interesting, Emma. Mary Todd Lincoln and Harriet Beecher Stowe."

"Right. She's the one who Lincoln called 'the little lady who started this big war.' "

The tallest model at the corner table starts giggling maniacally and slapping her long ebony thighs as though she's just heard the funniest punch line on earth. The photographer and the other model look on poker-faced as their cohort convulses into a choking fit. Now her colleague stands and starts pounding her between the shoulder blades while the photographer just sits there doing nothing. The first woman leaps out of her chair, spitting and gagging, while the second woman keeps bashing her in the back. Then the two of them go running hysterically across the foyer and into the bathroom. The man in the goatee is left alone at the table. He pulls out a French newspaper, flaps it open, takes a sip of ice water, and starts reading about the bad state of the world.

"What was that?" my daughter says.

"Something got caught in her pipes, I guess." My wife and son appear in the yellow archway of the dining room and spot the two of us at the table.

"Morning," she says as they approach the table.

"Morning," I say. "Did the wind keep you up last night? You were tossing and turning."

"It wasn't the wind," she says, pulling her chair out from the table.

. . . . .

The rest of our days down there were spent mostly strolling the white beach, reading Graham Greene novels, bodysurfing with my son; running into the little broken-down town for dinner some nights, walking the dirt backstreets, my wife taking photographs of hairless dogs staring down from barbed-wire-trimmed rooftops. Now and then we'd run into some friend or acquaintance from previous trips and sit with them in a café, sharing a beer. One blazing afternoon we visited the ruins and climbed the temple stairs where the dark blood of sacrificial hearts still stained the ancient stone. The issue about the "girlfriend" was dropped completely although some undeniable lurking enmity would pop up in weird moments; an argument over the use of the word *buscando*—a little flare-up about whether to leave the overhead fan running all night, squandering precious solar power. But, for the most part, we behaved decently toward each other and even held hands once or twice on our sunset walks, remembering the days we were seldom out of each other's sight and had no reason to doubt we would be forever in love.

. . . . .

On the return flight we sat four abreast with the aisle cut between us. Our daughter and I sat as a pair. Directly behind us was the couple from St. Paul again. The man had the window seat and made a cluster of soft guttural moans then went silent against the glass. Somewhere high above the Mississippi the woman let out a short anguished cry and leapt up to assist her husband. I unbuckled my safety belt and went back to see if I could help. The woman lay across the man's lap clutching her white handkerchief and trying to contain the horrible rush of brown fluid pouring down his chest. She was weeping and kissing his forehead which had turned as white as the handkerchief. His whole body seemed completely deflated and lay crushed against the glass as the sky raced by. She turned to me and her face was broken with grief. All the sorrow she'd been so heroically containing came flooding out. She moved aside and I took the man by the shoulders to pull him out into the aisle. As soon as I took hold of him I knew he was dead. I laid him down flat in the aisle, on his back. Another passenger who said he was a doctor knelt beside him and unbuttoned the man's shirt then began pressing and releasing his chest with both hands laid one on top of the other. I noticed a dark ruby ring on the doctor's finger with the emblem of a snake coiled around a cross. The woman kept hovering over the dead man's wide open eyes, speaking to him softly through her sobs. Flight attendants drew the curtains across the first-class section and spread blankets with the airline's logo over the dead man's legs and torso. The doctor switched to mouth-to-mouth resuscitation, using a small plastic device inserted in the dead man's mouth. When the doctor paused to take a break the woman implored him not to stop. The pilot announced over the

sound system that we would be making an emergency landing in
St. Louis and everyone was to bring their seats to an upright position and fasten their safety belts. The plane descended and circled
the city. The doctor's face now had a grim set to it although the
woman kept pleading for him to continue his efforts. As we landed
I could make out emergency life-support vehicles lining the run-
way with their yellow and red lights blinking. Young paramedics in
blue jumpsuits entered the plane and strapped the dead man to a
gurney. The wife and doctor followed them out. From the window
of the plane I could see the dead man's body jerking spasmodically
as they plugged it into the electric defibrillator. The arms flapped
helplessly on the black tarmac. They covered the dead man's face
with the blankets. The doctor put his arm around the widow's
shoulders. They took a step back from the body.

·　·　·　·　·

We drove in silence from the St. Paul airport when we finally made
it back to the house. The kids took off immediately to visit their
friends in the neighborhood. The dogs were glad to see us. The
canary flitted from one side of its cage to the other, causing its little brass bell to tinkle. The house felt cold and we turned the ther-
mostat up to 75. We hauled our carry-on luggage up the stairs to
the bedroom and dumped it on the floor. My cell phone started
ringing and blinking in the middle of the bed. Right where I'd
left it.

Screened-in Porch

He would smoke his black-market Cohiba on the screened-in porch right below her bedroom window and read *The Quarter Horse News* under a lamp spinning with moths on those warm prairie nights when Harleys roared up and down the river and teenage girls squealed from every passing coupe.

She would yell down to him that the smoke from his cigar was coming up through her open window and couldn't he go smoke the damn thing somewhere else and he would yell back, no, he was happy right where he was and if it bothered her so much she should close her damn window or go read in the kitchen.

Then she would start banging the hardback book she was reading on the hardwood floor, right next to her bed, right above his head and he knew it had to be something by Zola because Zola was all she read and he knew she read Zola because she knew Zola was way, way above his head.

Then, after a while of this: her banging the book; him blowing more smoke; he might wander off into the night, just out of spite; out of reach, across the dark lawn, trailing blue smoke over his stiff shoulders, and let the screen door slap behind him and maybe once glance back up at her yellowish light, remembering when she used to wonder if he was ever coming back and the terrible thrill of causing her to ache for his return.

Clarksville, Missouri

(Little Dixie Highway)

We stop along the Mississippi and walk down to a yellowish lime-stone monument dedicated to the flood relief volunteers of 1973. There are two hashmarks on the stone indicating the height of the floodwaters to have been over five feet. We climb up on the stone and sit, watching a family fish down along the bank of the mighty river. The man has a long line of purple monofilament wrapped around a Coke bottle which he keeps tugging and coiling while the woman fishes with a cheap, light spinning rod—the kind you can buy at Walgreens or Kmart. The kids dance up and down the shoreline throwing sticks and laughing wildly while their parents work with grim hard-set faces. They are obviously not fishing for pleasure. The woman almost lands what looks like an ugly pink carp but it pops off her line just as she drags it out of the water. She makes a dash for it but she's grossly out of shape and the fish escapes. She throws her arms up and turns to her husband, appeal-ing for sympathy but he's got his hands full hauling in an even big-ger and uglier carp. It splashes around in the shallows with its sucker mouth pumping for air and its big eye staring at the bright world. The woman makes a mad dash for the fish while her hus-band keeps tension on the line with the Coke bottle. She keeps try-ing to seize the carp by the neck but it squirms loose and flops back into the water. One of the kids runs up to his mother and hands her a long plank board which she grabs and proceeds to bash the fish over the head with, causing the line to break. The carp swims lazily off back into the black waters of the Mississippi with the kids chasing after it laughing hysterically. The man throws his hands up but makes no sound and starts wrapping the Coke bottle again with the slack line. The woman shrugs her shoulders and returns to her spinning reel; casts the heavy treble hook out far and hands the pole to her daughter. The man just stares off across the wide water. They've grown accustomed to bitter disappointment.

We ate together in small dark cafés lit by strings of electric chiles, facing out to the poor street; ribby dogs dodging handmade explosive motor scooters. Great smell of frying tortillas.

We strolled together down the white long beach past turtle eggs that hadn't hatched, pink plastic doll arms faded in the blazing sun, barnacled spike high heels washed in from Cuba or some distant pleasure ship.

We swam together in the green sea, rain beating us in the face, arms wide open to the tall black column cloud, her broad Midwestern smile.

Where are we now?

The Head Reflects

It's too bad but had I been whole; had I not been completely cut off as I was—as he found me in the ditch—we might have become great pals. Who knows? There seemed to be some immediate affinity there. But then again, I wasn't looking for friendship. My situation didn't allow it. A beast of burden was all I needed. Sad to say. That was it. Someone to simply get me from here to there. Selfish. Yes. But this was a desperate predicament I found myself in. A predicament I could have no more foreseen than one can name the date and place of one's death. Nights, I'd stare up at the sea of sky, searching for some sign in the heavens, some omen maybe. But from my odd position sunk deep in the ditch, only shards of galaxies revealed themselves: Tail of Scorpio. Leg of Pegasus. Orion's familiar belt. Nothing whole and clear, telling a story in three parts. Nothing so neat as that. Just fragments falling. Shooting stars. Satellites methodically tracking their looped orbits. Even sounds seemed broken and cut off from their source. Ducks winging in the dark with no destination. The whipping of wings. Opossum crashing blindly in the brush. For what? Once, a brindle bitch came by and sniffed at my severed neck then licked both my eyes but trotted off without so much as a nibble. Searching for fresher meat, I suppose. It wasn't the aloneness that gnawed away at me so much as the limbo. Not knowing where I'd wind up. Some orange Dumpster headed for the Ozarks maybe. It was right about then that the frail thought of friendship visited me in the ditch. I could feel it scratching around deep in the place where my chest used to be. The absence of a body is not something you get used to right away.

Bernalillo

In the summer of 1984, my father was killed in a small New Mexican town where the wide dusty streets are sunk three feet below modern sidewalk level. At the turn of the twentieth century this piece of city planning was designed to protect women in full skirts from the torrents of red mud cast up by buckboards and mules. Stumbling backwards out of the Cibola bar, my father tumbled off one of these high curbs directly into the path of an oncoming El Camino with neon blue lights silhouetting the lowered chassis. The anonymous driver never stopped. The bartender called the Albuquerque ambulance. When they loaded my father's mangled body on the gurney they asked him if he knew his name. "Just Sam," he said and then died right away. Ever since then I've had a stark terror of being blindsided by cars.

we sat around in rosy candlelight
exchanging tales of riptides
swimming too far out toward the reef
towed away in panic
underwater nightmares
breathless women
leaping off the fishing boat to take a leak
two hundred feet
of black Caribbean
straight down

all the while monster waves
crashing
just outside
green screens
white little crabs
frozen
poised sentinels
beside their tiny holes
translucent claws
raised to the salty air
and the razor-thin slice
of moon
just hanging there

Black Oath

I understand you've made giant strides toward your rehabilitation.

Who told you that?

I've heard it through the grapevine.

That's a song.

Well—

Did they say I'd repented? Down on my knees? Taken the oath?

They said you were behaving yourself.

That's nice.

Not biting anyone's ear off.

That's already been done.

Spitting in anyone's face.

God forbid.

You *are* interested in getting out of here, aren't you?

The outside is the same as the inside.

You can't be serious.

Try me.

Well, I was hoping we might come to some understanding.

Hope is for politicians.

I remember Paul very clearly. When he knew he was dying and you could see it in his eyes. Invited me into his tiny room. No more than eight by ten. Asked me to sit there with him. Just sit. And he sat very straight, in a straight-backed chair, hands on his knees; eyes calmly cast toward the floor. Asked me about my horses. That was the first thing. Wanted to know all about my horses. Said it was a good thing to follow your "passions," as he put it. "Passions." Said he remembered one day, riding. One day, years ago, sitting in some saddle. One moment when he felt himself to be. The subtle touch. The horse responding. The sensation of it. The power. Four days later Paul was dead. I counted them. Each and every one.

Things You Learn from Others

How to stop tucking your T-shirt into your underpants. How to drink from a cup without drooling. How to eat with a fork and not your hands. How to dry yourself off inside the shower so you don't get the floor wet. How to tie a half-hitch. How to make sure the disc plow overlaps the tire tread. How to tell when a colt is back at the knee. How to drive with one eye shut when you're skunk drunk. How to sleep all night in a ditch. How to sharpen a knife with a stone. How to gut a deer. How to read the flight of hawks and owls. How to release a greyhound in tall grass when you see the seed heads move in a silken wave. How to blindfold a spooky horse with burlap. How to do nothing but listen when someone wants to do nothing but talk.

What you don't learn, though, is how to protect others from your own manifestations of cruelty and malice which you've learned so insidiously through skin and blood and find impossible to shake free from no matter how much you'd like to be thought of as a decent, wholesome person.

Rape and Pillage

Let's go rape and pillage. You want to?

What? Have you lost your mind?

No, come on. One last time. What do you say?

Absolutely not! We gave that up. What's become of your short-term memory?

What? When?

Promises. Pledges. Resolutions.

Oh—those.

It was only day before yesterday— We swore on a stack of Bibles.

You swore.

So did you! I was your witness.

That wasn't me.

Day out of Days

I was right there, holding your skinny hand as you wept for mercy and forgiveness. Don't lie to me.

That's all in the past.

Two days ago!

So?

Don't be a fucking idiot! You want to start all that up again? All that—torment.

It was fun! Come on.

No! It wasn't fun. It was torture.

It was fun torturing others. You have to admit.

Don't make me sick.

Poking their eyeballs with fiery sticks.

Stop it!

Drawing and quartering.

Get away from me! Go walk on the other side of the field. I don't want to be anywhere near you.

You'll miss me.

Ha!

You will. You'll be walking over here and I'll be walking over there and you'll look across the wide field and yearn for my company. Wait and see.

Don't be stupid.

You will. You know you will. All the fun we've had over the years.

It wasn't fun! Get that out of your thick head. Fun is—Ferris wheels and cotton candy. I know what fun is.

All the dizzying ecstasy of absolute power. The debauchery. Looting things you'll never use.

All right! That's it. *I'm* going to go walk on the other side of the field and you stay here. You stay right here in your reverie and I'm going over there.

It'll be just the same.

What will?

The same as if *I* walked over there and you stayed over here. You'll still miss me. You'll still look across the field and yearn for my company.

Stop following me! You're worse than a dog.

I *am* a dog.

You're insane is what you are. Out of your tree! Doesn't that give you any kind of pause? The slightest little twinge of remorse?

Day out of Days

What?

That you're nuts! That once in the long-ago you might have had a glimmer of hope, a quick stab in the dark at sanity and self-respect. But no! You turned your back on it and walked away toward the roaring furnace. Never to return. Doesn't that make you wonder a little bit?

About what?

About what you've become!

I'm exactly where I want to be. Right by your side.

Stop following me!

Well, what're we going to do; stand around like a couple of fence-posts? I thought you wanted to take a walk.

I wanted to take a walk in peace! By myself. Alone with my thoughts.

How can you be alone with your thoughts?

Never mind. You're impossible. You know what I'm going to do? I'm going to tie you to that sycamore with my belt. That's what I'm going to do. I'll hang you from the thickest limb.

Oh, so now you're going to do me in? Is that it?

No, I'll hang you so your feet just barely touch the ground. Just enough so you can get periodic relief.

Oh, thanks very much.

Maybe I'll stone you like the good old days. Rocks and walnuts.

See? You can't give it up.

I'll keep you just barely alive. Hanging on by a thread.

What's the purpose of that?

Until you beg and twitch for mercy!

That'll never happen.

You'll see.

I'm tougher than I look.

You'll see. After three days your stomach will be eating your backbone.

I'm not buying into this transparent repentance of yours.

Of *mine*?

Of yours.

We confessed together!

Confessed? What am I now, Catholic or something?

Stop following me! Get away! Go somewhere else.

Day out of Days

Now you're hurting my feelings.

What feelings?

See?

I'm not talking to you anymore. I'm going to continue on my walk.
You're going to continue to follow me. You're going to continue to
hound and harangue me, like you always have, but I'm going to
completely ignore you.

That's not possible.

You'll see.

What will you do for inspiration?

You'll see.

Wait up!

should he head North
to her
climb into bed
with her
and would that make him soon forget
these morning nightmares
and random walks through woods
where he discovers nothing once again
but more of the same superstitions
traces of empty sagas
that don't work for luck
or anything else
you can put your finger on

would running up there
to her
straight North on 39
erase all that
or just create a whole new set
of lawless circumstances
he'd soon regret
and set him wondering why he'd ever left
the sweet sweet sunny South

stay
he said to himself
in the voice of a man
in the voice of a man inside his chest

who told him in stern tones
things were already changing
for the worse
and it was far far better
to stay right there
sitting in his faded armchair
than to risk the road again
and all its bitter disappointments

stay
and tough it out
between the cattle and the moon

but what if she goes off
and gives up the ghost
of him
forever
falls off the face of the earth
somewhere
without even a kiss good-bye
that would have to be worse
than risking the highway
one last time
surely
that would have to be much much worse

stay
and watch the next set of possibilities
arise
and fall away
what have you got to lose
but everything
piece by piece
everything
day by day

Lost Coin

My dad's grave gets no maintenance at the Veterans Cemetery. It sits out flat white in the red dust and hot Sangre de Cristo winds. In winter you can't even find it in the blue banks of snow. You go kicking around through powder as though searching for lost coins. Your hands get red and numb, digging. Your breath grows short from the altitude. You end up drinking.

Once, a flaming young Spanish woman came right up to me in a bar and simply declared that her grandfather, Filiberto Lujan, occupied the grave right next to my father's. She quickly vanished before I could fall in love.

Circling

Sitting here. Watching my heart pump in my right ankle. Bump, bump. Next door, a woman cackles madly. Entertaining her children. Making up crazy voices. Changing faces. She runs from room to room. The kids are going nuts trying to catch her.

You circle all around your life, but do you find it? You circle from above. Like a hawk. Below the ozone. Looking down. On the hunt. From Pecos to Healdsburg. Carlsbad to Reno. Do you find it?

Sitting here in a straight-backed chair. Staring down. Pump, pump. Looking just like the same panicked kid from your Duarte yearbook. The year you never graduated. Am I looking? Am I seeing this? The sun lighting up my naked leg. Wrinkled veins. All the coarse hairs swirling around my red horse scars. Battles. Knives and guns. The kids next door. Screaming. Can't tell if they're happy or scared.

You circle all around your life, but do you find it?

there's a man in a pay phone
dramatically lit
he's saving himself
for his last cigarette

his face changes color
his hand's dripping wet
as he digs for a quarter
and comes up with ten cent

Back in the Woods

I'm back.

Well, look at you. I guess you're back.

Yeah—I'm back.

Well, well, well— For how long this time?

Um— Don't know.

Right. So— How was it out there on the dumb American highway, days on end? Have any revelations?

No—

Epiphanies?

No—

Divine manifestations?

Look—

What? You have some sort of confession to make?

Day out of Days

No— Why?

Guilty conscience?

About what?

How many pathetic women did you leave out there—dazed and bewildered, turning in circles?

Can't we just—

What?

Get along?

Depends.

On what?

Your availability.

I'm going to stay here for at least a week.

Not that.

What then?

Never mind.

What?

I have to go down to the post office.

Wait a second—

What?

I don't know. I just get back and now you have to go down to the post office?

Yeah. Life goes on.

I know but—

What?

I don't know—

Oh— Would you mind moving your Chevy off the lawn, please? It kills the grass.

Sure. Where do you want it?

I don't care—down by the lake, maybe. No—not down by the lake. I don't want to be looking at it in the morning, out the kitchen window.

Where then?

Put it way back deep in the woods. Somewhere. Back where I can't see it.

Holyoke

Somebody's shooting deep in the woods. Wind is out of the north and somebody's out there shooting. A hawk struggles through it, ducking and diving, doing his best. Two loons. Wind makes the water race in dark bars. Across the lake somebody keeps shooting. Light keeps shifting. You can feel all kinds of weather in it. Weather from far off, rolling in. The gun makes the dog cringe. Dog crinkles up with every bang. Boat knocking up against the dock; tethered to it, just rocking. Water slapping the aluminum hull in little claps. Faraway thunder. You can see it coming.

She sits down beside me now with a big white bowl of peaches in her lap. She makes my heart sing. Her lap and her peaches. Gun keeps going off deep in the birch. Saplings squeak. Tamarack. Black butterfly struggles in the wind. Dog keeps her one good eye on the loons. Red sumac. Indian plumage. Shoshone. Arapaho. Someone keeps shooting. Far off. Must be just practice, for something big. Something coming up.

One Stone

when I dug the deep grave
for her father's body
through pure glacial sand
I came across one stone
at the very bottom
perfectly smooth
and deep dark orange
ripe as a fallen apricot

I brought it to the surface
kept it on my dashboard for miles
rattling around
wherever I went

she never knew where it came from
never asked
I never said

Regrets of the Head

I do regret not opening up my eyes and allowing him to see into me, just that once. I do regret that now. I should have been more generous. If I had it to do over again perhaps I would. What in the world did I have to lose? I'd already lost my entire body. What was left? Fear I guess. Of what? Of him seeing me? I guess. But what? What in me could have been so terrible? So impossible to behold. God knows I carried it around inside me all my many days. Carried it like a faithful slave. But he was a different kind of man than me. Such a gentle soul. Kind. You could see it in his eyes. Not a mean bone in his body. Kind enough to stop on his Sunday walk and pick me up at least. Carry me all that ways. He wasn't obliged to do that. He wasn't under any orders. He just found it in the goodness of his heart. The goodness of his heart. And mine had long left me. Nothing there but this gruesome head. It must have been truly terrifying to him. I doubt he ever even brought himself to tell the story. Tell the tale. Who in the wide world would ever believe a thing like that? A head in a ditch that talks? That pleads for forgiveness. That moans and groans with self-pity. At least that part of it's over. No more bobbing to the surface. I wonder about him, though, sometimes. My last contact with the tribe. I wonder if he ever made it back to the wife. The little lady. The love of his life. Or if he's still wandering up and down those roads, poking at things in the ditches; talking to trees. I should have let him see into my eyes. Just that once. It might have been a help to him. It might have brought him some peace. To know the two of us were entirely separate. Complete opposite ends of the stick. There was never any danger of him becoming me. Falling into the pit. He was entirely himself. It was me that was split. It was only me.

Indio, California

Floating flat on my back in the bare night sky, rippling yellow pool lights in stripes across the deep end. Staring up at the wide splash of desert stars as my son tries to sink himself to the bottom, exhaling all his wind, like he might become a dark boulder. He won't sink. He can't get himself to sink no matter what he tries. He's like a dry stick, blond hair streaming out as though he might have fallen from this very sky. I remember the two of us jumping into the bass pond on the ranch back home. Middle of summer. Temperature up in the high nineties. We were diving down deep into the slimy green water trying to retrieve an old sunken raft. I came up gasping. That was the very first indication I had something seriously wrong with my heart: Desperate breath. Ache in the armpit. Ropes in the neck. The panic, although I kept it hidden from my son. He kept right on diving while I pulled myself onshore, face-down, spitting dirt.

Now the clear world floats way above. Cassiopeia in a perfect 3. Desert wind. Us below. Lipitor. Zetia. Ramipril. If this were 1876, I'd be dead in a heartbeat.

Wisconsin Wilderness

"Funny how some little impulse, some notion like that can pop up and here you find yourself suddenly snowshoeing across the Wisconsin wilderness in dead winter." This was the thought that came to him in the midst of his heart pounding, breath gasping, eyes locked down on the brand new pair of bright orange Atlas snowshoes he'd bought at Fleet Farm. He'd seen a pair just like it hanging in the back porch of his brother-in-law's place, prompting this whole new adventure. The real spur, of course, was his little "almost" heart-attack experience going back to October on the West Coast; that was the real catalyst—"an event like that"; "out of the blue." One minute he's eating sushi on Sutter Street, the next he's collapsed at the bottom of the glass steps of the hotel, tourists brushing past him with their black luggage. None of the classic symptoms; no pressing pain in the chest, no stabbing in the left arm, just flat out of air and the back of his neck tied up in deep knots. It seemed to him he still hadn't quite caught up to the full impact of it. Caution regarding the unseeable organs was something that had never occurred to him. You can only imagine the heart inside there, pounding away in its red cage. He'd seen the ghostly tomographic images after the failed stress test but they resembled nothing like his mental image of a heart—*his* heart. The gangly left anterior descending artery dancing out across the page like some Japanese fighting dragon with two very noticeable constrictions, thin as horsehair. But to actually feel himself to be the possessor of a diseased heart was almost impossible. His new idea now was that he thought he needed to push himself physically to some brink to find out exactly where the boundary was. He'd followed all the doctor's admonitions about not smoking, avoiding fried foods, stressful situations (that one seemed next to impossible since the very knowledge of his new condition seemed to turn every situation into a possible threat). He religiously downed his daily dose of five colorful pills: anticoagulant pills, cholesterol reduction pills, ramipril, Zetia, a specially coated 325-milligram. aspirin and now, here he was intentionally going out of his way to exercise and raise his heart rate like some aerobic moron—the kind of dutiful citizen he used to hold in highest contempt. He could hardly believe his about-face. What a man would do when he had a gun to his head. How he could suddenly forsake his most sacred obsessions, abandoning entire aspects of character he had taken to be immutable. He had been a solid, deep-inhaling smoker since he was twelve, pilfering Chesterfield butts from his old man's ashtray. That pitted musky teakwood memento hand-carved in the Philippines in the figure of a native man squatting in his loincloth gently embracing a chicken in a wicker basket. It had been part of his father's booty brought back from World War II in a green army duffel and shuffled from house to house during his peripatetic childhood. The black bowl of the thing always overflowing with half-smoked delicious butts he'd carefully straighten and preserve in a Yuban coffee can buried out behind the tangerine tree. At night, from the blue foothills, he would draw deep gusts of smoke, squatting in the same posture as the little native man; staring deep into the broad valley, eyes tracing the snaking car lights along US 66. He became dizzy with nicotine and imagination. By the age of sixteen he was totally addicted and indoctrinated into the strong belief that manhood and smoking were synonymous. There was nothing he did without a cigarette clenched between his fingers or his teeth: mowing lawns, working under cars, saddling horses, even necking with girls, the ubiquitous cigarette became a prop of necessity. Now he'd actually managed to cold-turkey for

Day out of Days

two and a half months. He could still feel his tongue yearning for the bright sting of smoke.

He remembered the collegiate-looking doctor in a red bow tie hovering over him the morning after the stent procedure saying, "You've already gone twenty-four hours without one cigarette. Why don't you just try stopping altogether?" He remembered wondering how many times the doctor had used this exact same ploy on other victims; hitting a man when he's down. He had flopped the hospital sheets back away from his legs and saw the cloudy deep bruises turning a ghastly green on either side of his crotch where they'd inserted the long catheter, probing it up through the artery, searching for the dangerously collapsed areas. He remembered watching the eyes of the surgeon as he worked. The eyes following the path of the catheter on an overhead monitor while the hands manipulated the journey in some strange dance of high technology and raw human coordination. On the morning after, there wasn't much pain at all. Just a deep vague ache like what happens when you get hit with a hardball in the soft inner part of the bicep. An extremely black nurse came in with his street clothes draped over her left shoulder. She laid them out on a metal chair and told him he could get dressed now, they were releasing him. He remembered this woman from the day before with another nurse who could have been her twin. They kept firing questions at him in a singsong way as they prepared him for the procedure in a small curtained anteroom: "Where's your home, honey? Where's your family? What kind of work do you do?" None of these questions made any sense to him in the face of his current health predicament so he said nothing and meekly smiled at them as though he'd temporarily lost his mind. He took out his Wisconsin driver's license and told them they could take down all the information off that. That was the best he could do at the moment. He hadn't brought anything with him. This whole heart business had caught him completely off-guard. He'd just climbed into his white Suburban and driven straight from downtown San Fran-

272

cisco, across the Oakland Bay Bridge right directly to the clinic, halfway praying he wouldn't have a heart attack in the middle of traffic. He thought that might be a terrible way to die. Reminded him of that old Beatles song where someone from the House of Lords dies at a traffic light. All kinds of random dumb things were going through his head and he panicked at the idea that his mind was not going to come to the aid of his body; that these two aspects of himself were, in fact, completely divorced. One of the extremely black nurses cast him a wry grin and said, "Don't worry, darlin', we'll be your family if you haven't got one." He felt strangely reassured by this. After he'd stripped down and managed to drape the open-backed blue hospital smock around himself and push his cold feet into the ridiculous terry-cloth slippers they'd provided, the nurses ushered him out through the curtains to a chrome gurney. He remembered a certain sense of humiliation climbing up on the thing with his bare ass sticking out and then lying down on his back seeing his white chicken legs ending in the silly slippers. Now a set of male nurses took over, outfitted in green pajamas, white shower caps, sheer latex gloves, and plastic baggies encasing their feet. They had the physiques of men in their mid- to late thirties who avidly work out with weights as though terrified of suddenly losing their youth. It bothered him slightly that such personal concerns outside their medical profession could distract them from the business at hand; that they might easily mess up a minor detail in the procedure that would prove fatal or worse— make a cabbage out of him, on life support. He tried to tell himself calmly that none of this mattered; he was in the hands of fate. His mind wouldn't listen.

They wheeled him into the operating room and parked him under a bank of intense halogen lights. One of them depressed a brake and tested the gurney to see if it might somehow run off on its own but it held firm. Large monitor screens loomed down at angles from the ceiling. One of the green male nurses explained in a very flat even voice that he was going to attach a sterile bag around the penis and testicles in case there might be some involuntary urination during the process, in which case he should feel free to cut loose. He remembered nodding to the nurse as though giving permission and then felt his sexual parts being collected as someone might gather up plums at the grocery store and stuff them into a bag for weighing. He wondered how many times in a week this nurse might repeat this process and then he wondered again about the body-building. The idea that he might piss himself in front of total strangers bothered him more than the possibility that something could go terribly wrong in the catheter's sojourn into the long and winding cardiovascular system. A chunk of plaque might easily chip off and rush directly to the heart or the artery might entirely reject the implanted stent and the whole game would be over, just like that. The whole game.

"Can't believe that was—how many months ago and here I am now— Snow. Ice. Subzero. Maybe it's not such a great idea to push this thing. You don't really know what you're doing, do you? Sucking in cold air can't be so good for an ailing heart. What if something actually happened— I mean out here in the middle of nowhere? Who's going to find you? First of all you'd probably freeze to death if the heart didn't finish you off right away. It would take days for them to track you down. You never even told anybody you were coming up here. Very smart. There you'd be—stiff as a board, wildlife sniffing all around your corpse. Fox. Badger. Great horned owls landing on your chest in the night, pecking at your eyes. Critters shitting all over your sorry self—what's left of it. Who's going to know? You could lay out here for weeks before they'd track you down." He kept moving; shuffling through the crusted snow like some preprogrammed android. He had no real plan. He wasn't counting his pulse or measuring miles or going about this in any sort of scientific way. He was just crashing ahead through the cedars and pines, hoping he wasn't going in circles like the proverbial lost desert rat. What was he actually trying to prove? he asked himself but no answer came back. Nothing but the pounding blood in his head, the gasping breath. "This was stupid," he began to chant. "This is really dumb." But nothing in him stopped. His legs kept churning; his arms kept swinging. He tried returning to his original idea—that it might just be possible to find the real threshold where the body gave out entirely. But then, how was that supposed to work exactly? Would he be able to sense the very early stages of a full-blown heart attack through some mysterious prescience he couldn't assume he possessed and then draw back and save himself with a raw act of will which he also found deeply absent? In fact, suddenly, nothing in him seemed deliberate. It was as though he had become possessed by a maniac intent on provoking calamity and he was just along for the ride. He charged on, sweat pouring down his ribs and the insides of his thighs. The back of his skull felt like it might blow off. In the distance someone was practicing with a high-powered rifle; the dull thud of the repercussion drilling through his chest, straight to the heart. Now the whole world seemed to be about nothing but the heart. Like when a baby is born into the family all you can see is babies. Or dying—someone dying in the hospital—but that wasn't right. The rifle went off again in a staccato flutter. His heart seemed to match the report, thumping up through the stem of his neck into both temples. The air was so cold the moisture from his eyes froze them shut when he blinked then cracked back open with a sting. He was losing sensation in both thumbs even though he'd pulled Thinsulate gloves on over thinner wool ones then encased both hands in puffy red mittens. The rifle kept on thudding in regular intervals. He wondered who it was who could be so utterly bored that they needed to come out in weather like this and shoot random holes in a pine tree. But then, who could be so out of their minds as to lash snowshoes to their feet and slam through cold woods pretending to be a man on a mission?

A slim plane silently etched its way across the blank sky. He kept marching far below. He thought about the passengers at twenty thousand feet, heading somewhere—somewhere warm and tropical. Mexico, maybe. The thought of Mexico always warmed his heart. There it was again—the heart. Coming up again. How many aspects to it? How could something so animal become fractured into so many parts? Montezuma. Rivers of blood pouring down the halls. Glimmering shrines to the Dreaded Duality. Two monstrous eyes encrusted with precious stones, girdled with serpents and clawed lizards, necklaces of silver hearts and below, dripping in golden chains, the very human hearts freshly torn from the hairless chests of teenage children—ripped out of them with obsidian daggers in the shapes of eagles and dogs. The walls and floors of the oratory were so splashed and encrusted with blood they had turned a deep ebony black, throbbing in the pit of the jungle. He marched on through ice.

Distant Songs of Madmen

Sometimes, lying propped up against the half-opened window, a great calm would come over him listening to the distant songs of madmen moaning in the streets below. He could never make out the exact words but melody lines would weave together; weave in and out of other sounds like faraway sirens, trains, TVs from other open windows, babbling news. There was some peace in the distance, in the listening, in the longing wails impossible to be answered. Peace of a kind that had no ambition, no plan, no political motive. Peace for its own sake.

these pills
the orange one
blue
yellow
two white ones
in the palm of your hand
lined up across your lifeline
to ward off what
to delay
to prolong
to keep away
what
until one day you just fall down flat
and the family starts calling itself on the phone
the network begins
he's down again and broken
different bones
can't remember shit
wanders off now to different towns
he thinks he had a past in
can't keep him in his room
got a call from Lubbock
Missing Persons
man couldn't pronounce his name

said it sounded like
Chambers maybe but slurred
next morning he was gone
out the open window
no trace
no tracks
of any kind

Rogers, Arkansas

(Highway 62)

Man finally makes it to the shore of the lake with the severed head teetering above him the whole way. He can hardly wait to get rid of it. This whole ordeal. The burning pain in the back of his neck. The trembling in his shoulders and arms. Why should he have to endure this torture? For what? He stands there panting, staring out across the flat green water to the cattails on the opposite shore. A great blue heron struts then freezes on one leg; its wild yellow eye staring back, over all that space. "Right here," the head tells him. "This is perfect. Right here."

"What do you want me to do?" asks the man with a helpless whine.

"Just toss me in," says the head. "Just give me the old heave-ho!" The man lowers the head to his waist and stares into the face of it. The eyes are still shut tight; squinting with that rictus that must have been its last quick moment before the sword came down. The man has a sudden wish that he could see into the eyes of the head for just one flashing second. That he might see the person behind the voice. That he might know something, some small inkling of the nature of the head.

"Do you think you could open your eyes for me? Just once?" asks the man.

"No," says the head, without hesitation.

"Why?" asks the man.

"Because you wouldn't be able to take it," answers the head. The man quickly tosses the head straight up in the air, without knowing why. It's as though his whole body has reacted with an electric jolt and jettisoned something poisonous. The heron takes off on the far side of the lake, pumping its enormous wings in slow motion. When the tumbling head smacks down into the flat green water it immediately bobs back up and starts swirling in tight circles like a volleyball cast overboard in the open sea. The man makes a little gasp as he watches the head twist and roll through the expanding ripples, drifting farther and farther from shore. The man takes three quick steps into the water as though he might swim after it and catch hold of its black, curly hair but the man stops short and just watches the head floating away. The shadow of the great blue heron passes over the man, who can't take his eyes off the head. Then the head just sinks and never comes back up. It just sinks like that. As the man watches intensely for any sign of its reappearance, the green water slowly heals itself back to stillness. Smooth and flat. A painted turtle pops its yellow nose up on a lily pad. The man waits there a long, long time, knee deep in the water, searching for any sign of the head, but nothing comes up. Finally, the man turns his back on the lake and wades to shore. He stands there dripping for a while, afraid to turn around. He can hear the drone of the highway, far off. The chimes of the church. He can see the gray dot of the heron, sailing away. He opens his mouth but nothing comes out. No expression of any kind.

Gracias

What little town was that where we drove for miles weaving through hills and hills of olive groves poured out like little oceans and arrived at a tall gray pensión with an ancient church right across and canaries singing in every window from every balcony and old pudgy women in black ankle-length dresses hobbling along and the two of us, I remember, walking hand in hand with our children, talking of living somewhere idyllic just like this somewhere suspended in time and then all of us brought to a stop by a pianist practicing some lovely lilting waltz outside a window with iron bars in a narrow backstreet and we all just stood there entranced and applauded from the street when it ended for the unseen player and from somewhere deep inside the thick stucco walls, very faintly, came a woman's voice, very very soft, and the voice said "Gracias," and we walked on.

That was one of those days I remember.

ALSO BY SAM SHEPARD

BURIED CHILD

A newly revised edition of an American classic, Sam Shepard's Pulitzer Prize–winning *Buried Child* is as fierce and unforgettable as it was when it was first produced more than twenty-five years ago. A scene of madness greets Vince and his girlfriend as they arrive at the squalid farmhouse of Vince's hard-drinking grandparents, who seem to have no idea who he is. Nor does his father, Tilden, a hulking former all-American football player, or his uncle, who has lost one of his legs to a chain saw. Only the memory of an unwanted child, buried in an undisclosed location, can hope to deliver this family from its sin.

Drama/978-0-307-27497-7

ALSO AVAILABLE

Cruising Paradise, 978-0-679-74217-3
God of Hell, 978-1-4000-9651-0
Great Dream of Heaven, 978-0-375-70452-9
Kicking a Dead Horse, 978-0-307-38682-3
The Late Henry Moss, Eyes for Consuela, When the World Was Green, 978-1-4000-3079-8
Simpatico, 978-0-679-76317-8
States of Shock, Far North, 978-0-679-74218-0
Tooth of Crime, 978-0-307-27498-4
The Unseen Hand, 978-0-679-76789-3

VINTAGE BOOKS
Available at your local bookstore, or visit
www.randomhouse.com